The Boy Without a Flag

Tales of the South Bronx

THE BOY WITHOUT A FLAG

by

Abraham Rodriguez, Jr.

MILKWEED EDITIONS

"Babies" was originally published in Best Stories from New Writers *(Writers Digest Books, 1989). "Elba" was originally published by* Story *magazine.*

The Boy Without a Flag

© 1992, Stories by Abraham Rodriguez, Jr.
© 1992, Drawings by R. W. Scholes

Printed in the United States of America.
Published in 1992 by Milkweed Editions.

Milkweed Editions
528 Hennepin Avenue, Suite 505
Minneapolis, Minnesota 55403
Books may be ordered from the above address.

ISBN 0-915943-74-3

95 94 93   4 3 2

We are grateful for the generous sponsorship of *The Boy Without a Flag* by the Cowles Media Foundation.

Publication of this and other Milkweed books is made possible by grant support from the Literature Program of the National Endowment for the Arts, the Dayton Hudson Foundation for Dayton's and Target Stores, Ecolab Foundation, the First Bank System Foundation, the General Mills Foundation, the I. A. O'Shaughnessy Foundation, the Jerome Foundation, The McKnight Foundation, the Andrew W. Mellon Foundation, the Minnesota State Arts Board through an appropriation by the Minnesota Legislature, the Northwest Area Foundation, and by the support of generous individuals.

Library of Congress Cataloging-in-Publication Data

Rodriguez, Abraham, Jr., 1961-
    The boy without a flag : tales of the South Bronx /
by Abraham Rodriguez, Jr.
        p.   cm.
    ISBN 0-915943-74-3 (paper)
    1. Puerto Ricans—New York (N.Y.)—Fiction.   2. Bronx
(New York, N.Y.)—Fiction.   I. Title.
PS3568.034876B69 1992
813'.54—dc20   91-45672
                                                                      CIP

To my parents
—still the best

The Boy Without a Flag

The Boy Without a Flag 11
No More War Games 31
Babies 45
Birthday Boy 61
Short Stop 75
The Lotto 87
Elba 105

The Boy Without a Flag

"The language of the beaten nation is not forgotten in our ears tonight."

—John Dos Passos, *The Big Money*

THE BOY WITHOUT A FLAG

— To Ms. Linda Falcón,
wherever she is

Swirls of dust danced in the beams of sunlight that came
through the tall windows, the buzz of voices resounding in the
stuffy auditorium. Mr. Rios stood by our Miss Colon, hovering
as if waiting to catch her if she fell. His pale mouse features
looked solemnly dutiful. He was a versatile man, doubling as
English teacher and gym coach. He was only there because
of Miss Colon's legs. She was wearing her neon pink nylons.
Our favorite.

We tossed suspicious looks at the two of them. Miss
Colon would smirk at Edwin and me, saying, "Hey, face front,"
but Mr. Rios would glare. I think he knew that we knew what
he was after. We knew, because on Fridays, during our free
period when we'd get to play records and eat stale pretzel
sticks, we would see her way in the back by the tall windows,
sitting up on a radiator like a schoolgirl. There would be a
strange pinkness on her high cheekbones, and there was Mr.
Rios, sitting beside her, playing with her hand. Her face, so
thin and girlish, would blush. From then on, her eyes, very

close together like a cartoon rendition of a beaver's, would avoid us.

Miss Colon was hardly discreet about her affairs. Edwin had first tipped me off about her love life after one of his lunchtime jaunts through the empty hallways. He would chase girls and toss wet bathroom napkins into classrooms where kids in the lower grades sat, trapped. He claimed to have seen Miss Colon slip into a steward's closet with Mr. Rios and to have heard all manner of sounds through the thick wooden door, which was locked (he tried it). He had told half the class before the day was out, the boys sniggering behind grimy hands, the girls shocked because Miss Colon was married, so married that she even brought the poor unfortunate in one morning as a kind of show-and-tell guest. He was an untidy dark-skinned Puerto Rican type in a colorful dashiki. He carried a paper bag that smelled like glue. His eyes seemed sleepy, his Afro an uncombed Brillo pad. He talked about protest marches, the sixties, the importance of an education. Then he embarrassed Miss Colon greatly by disappearing into the coat closet and falling asleep there. The girls, remembering him, softened their attitude toward her indiscretions, defending her violently. "Face it," one of them blurted out when Edwin began a new series of Miss Colon tales, "she married a bum and needs to find true love."

"She's a slut, and I'm gonna draw a comic book about her," Edwin said, hushing when she walked in through the door. That afternoon, he showed me the first sketches of what would later become a very popular comic book entitled "Slut At The Head Of The Class." Edwin could draw really well, but his stories were terrible, so I volunteered to do the writing. In no time at all, we had three issues circulating under desks and hidden in notebooks all over the school. Edwin secretly ran off close to a hundred copies on a copy machine in the main office after school. It always amazed me how copies of our comic kept popping up in the unlikeliest places. I saw them on

12   *The Boy Without a Flag*

spurned. I didn't even mention that my fascination with Adolf led to my writing a biography of him, a book report one hundred and fifty pages long. It got an A-plus. Miss Colon stapled it to the bulletin board right outside the classroom, where it was promptly stolen.

"So, what makes you want to be a writer?" Miss Colon asked me quietly one day, when Edwin and I, always the helpful ones, volunteered to assist her in getting the classroom spiffed up for a Halloween party.

"I don't know. I guess my father," I replied, fiddling with plastic pumpkins self-consciously while images of my father began parading through my mind.

When I think back to my earliest image of my father, it is one of him sitting behind a huge rented typewriter, his fingers clacking away. He was a frustrated poet, radio announcer, and even stage actor. He had sent for diplomas from fly-by-night companies. He took acting lessons, went into broadcasting, even ended up on the ground floor of what is now Spanish radio, but his family talked him out of all of it. "You should find yourself real work, something substantial," they said, so he did. He dropped all those dreams that were never encouraged by anyone else and got a job at a Nedick's on Third Avenue. My pop the counterman.

Despite that, he kept writing. He recited his poetry into a huge reel-to-reel tape deck that he had, then he'd play it back and sit like a critic, brow furrowed, fingers stroking his lips. He would record strange sounds and play them back to me at outrageous speeds, until I believed that there were tiny people living inside the machine. I used to stand by him and watch him type, his black pompadour spilling over his forehead. There was energy pulsating all around him, and I wanted a part of it.

I was five years old when I first sat in his chair at the kitchen table and began pushing down keys, watching the letters magically appear on the page. I was entranced. My fascination with the typewriter began at that point. By the time I was ten, I was writing war stories, tales of pain and pathos culled from the piles of comic books I devoured. I wrote unreadable novels. With illustrations. My father wasn't impressed. I guess he was hard to impress. My terrific grades did not faze him, nor the fact that I was reading books as fat as milk crates. My unreadable novels piled up. I brought them to him at night to see if he would read them, but after a week of waiting I found them thrown in the bedroom closet, unread. I felt hurt and rejected, despite my mother's kind words. "He's just too busy to read them," she said to me one night when I mentioned it to her. He never brought them up, even when I quietly took them out of the closet one day or when he'd see me furiously hammering on one of his rented machines. I would tell him I wanted to be a writer, and he would smile sadly and pat my head, without a word.

"You have to find something serious to do with your life," he told me one night, after I had shown him my first play, eighty pages long. What was it I had read that got me into writing a play? Was it Arthur Miller? Oscar Wilde? I don't remember, but I recall my determination to write a truly marvelous play about combat because there didn't seem to be any around.

"This is fun as a hobby," my father said, "but you can't get serious about this." His demeanor spoke volumes, but I couldn't stop writing. Novels, I called them, starting a new one every three days. The world was a blank page waiting for my words to recreate it, while the real world remained cold and lonely. My schoolmates didn't understand any of it, and because of the fat books I carried around, I was held in some fear. After all, what kid in his right mind would read a book if it wasn't assigned? I was sick of kids coming up to me and saying, "Gaw, lookit tha fat book. Ya teacha make ya read tha?" (No, I'm just reading it.) The kids would look at me as if I had just crawled out of a sewer. "Ya crazy, man." My father seemed to share that opinion. Only my teachers understood and encouraged my reading, but my father seemed to want something else from me.

Now, he treated me like an idiot for not knowing what imperialism was. He berated my books and one night handed me a copy of a book about Albizu Campos, the Puerto Rican revolutionary. I read it through in two sittings.

"Some of it seems true," I said.

"Some of it?" my father asked incredulously. "After what they did to him, you can sit there and act like a Yankee flag-waver?"

I watched that Yankee flag making its way up to the stage over indifferent heads, my father's scowling face haunting me, his words resounding in my head.

"Let me tell you something," my father sneered. "In school, all they do is talk about George Washington, right? The first president? The father of democracy? Well, he had slaves. We had our own Washington, and ours had real teeth."

As Old Glory reached the stage, a general clatter ensued.

"We had our own revolution," my father said, "and the United States crushed it with the flick of a pinkie."

Miss Marti barked her royal command. Everyone rose up to salute the flag.

Except me. I didn't get up. I sat in my creaking seat, hands on my knees. A girl behind me tapped me on the back. "Come on, stupid, get up." There was a trace of concern in her voice. I didn't move.

Miss Colon appeared. She leaned over, shaking me gently. "Are you sick? Are you okay?" Her soft hair fell over my neck like a blanket.

"No," I replied.

"What's wrong?" she asked, her face growing stern. I was beginning to feel claustrophobic, what with everyone standing all around me, bodies like walls. My friend Edwin, hand on his heart, watched from the corner of his eye. He almost looked envious, as if he wished he had thought of it. Murmuring voices around me began reciting the Pledge while Mr. Rios appeared, commandingly grabbing me by the shoulder and pulling me out of my seat into the aisle. Miss Colon was beside him, looking a little apprehensive.

"What is wrong with you?" he asked angrily. "You know you're supposed to stand up for the Pledge! Are you religious?"

"No," I said.

"Then what?"

"I'm not saluting that flag," I said.

"What?"

"I said, I'm not saluting that flag."

"Why the...?" He calmed himself; a look of concern flashed over Miss Colon's face. "Why not?"

"Because I'm Puerto Rican. I ain't no American. And I'm not no Yankee flag-waver."

"You're supposed to salute the flag," he said angrily, shoving one of his fat fingers in my face. "You're not supposed to make up your own mind about it. You're supposed to do as you are told."

"I thought I was free," I said, looking at him and at Miss Colon.

"You are," Miss Colon said feebly. "That's why you should salute the flag."

"But shouldn't I do what I feel is right?"

"You should do what you are told!" Mr. Rios yelled into my face. "I'm not playing no games with you, mister. You hear that music? That's the anthem. Now you go stand over there and put your hand over your heart." He made as if to grab my hand, but I pulled away.

"No!" I said sharply. "I'm not saluting that crummy flag! And you can't make me, either. There's nothing you can do about it."

"Oh yeah?" Mr. Rios roared. "We'll see about that!"

"Have you gone crazy?" Miss Colon asked as he led me

away by the arm, down the hallway, where I could still hear the strains of the anthem. He walked me briskly into the principal's office and stuck me in a corner. "You stand there for the rest of the day and see how you feel about it," he said viciously. "Don't you even think of moving from that spot!"

I stood there for close to two hours or so. The principal came and went, not even saying hi or hey or anything, as if finding kids in the corners of his office was a common occurrence. I could hear him talking on the phone, scribbling on pads, talking to his secretary. At one point I heard Mr. Rios outside in the main office.

"Some smart-ass. I stuck him in the corner. Thinks he can pull that shit. The kid's got no respect, man. I should get the chance to teach him some."

"Children today have no respect," I heard Miss Marti's reptile voice say as she approached, heels clacking like gunshots. "It has to be forced upon them."

She was in the room. She didn't say a word to the principal, who was on the phone. She walked right over to me. I could hear my heart beating in my ears as her shadow fell over me. Godzilla over Tokyo.

"Well, have you learned your lesson yet?" she asked, turning me from the wall with a finger on my shoulder. I stared at her without replying. My face burned, red hot. I hated it.

"You think you're pretty important, don't you? Well, let me tell you, you're nothing. You're not worth a damn. You're just a snotty-nosed little kid with a lot of stupid ideas." Her eyes bored holes through me, searing my flesh. I felt as if I were going to cry. I fought the urge. Tears rolled down my face anyway. They made her smile, her chapped lips twisting upwards like the mouth of a lizard.

"See? You're a little baby. You don't know anything, but you'd better learn your place." She pointed a finger in my face.

"You do as you're told if you don't want big trouble. Now go back to class."

Her eyes continued to stab at me. I looked past her and saw Edwin waiting by the office door for me. I walked past her, wiping at my face. I could feel her eyes on me still, even as we walked up the stairs to the classroom. It was close to three already, and the skies outside the grated windows were cloudy.

"Man," Edwin said to me as we reached our floor, "I think you're crazy."

The classroom was abuzz with activity when I got there. Kids were chattering, getting their windbreakers from the closet, slamming their chairs up on their desks, filled with the euphoria of soon-home. I walked quietly over to my desk and took out my books. The other kids looked at me as if I were a ghost.

I went through the motions like a robot. When we got downstairs to the door, Miss Colon, dismissing the class, pulled me aside, her face compassionate and warm. She squeezed my hand.

"Are you okay?"

I nodded.

"That was a really crazy stunt there. Where did you get such an idea?"

I stared at her black flats. She was wearing tan panty hose and a black miniskirt. I saw Mr. Rios approaching with his class.

"I have to go," I said, and split, running into the frigid breezes and the silver sunshine.

At home, I lay on the floor of our living room, tapping my open notebook with the tip of my pen while the Beatles blared from my father's stereo. I felt humiliated and alone. Miss Marti's reptile face kept appearing in my notebook, her voice intoning, "Let me tell you, you're nothing." Yeah, right. Just what horrible hole did she crawl out of? Were those people really Puerto Ricans? Why should a Puerto Rican salute an American flag?

I put the question to my father, strolling into his bedroom, a tiny M-1 rifle that belonged to my G.I. Joe strapped to my thumb.

"Why?" he asked, loosening the reading glasses that were perched on his nose, his newspaper sprawled open on the bed before him, his cigarette streaming blue smoke. "Because we are owned, like cattle. And because nobody has any pride in their culture to stand up for it."

I pondered those words, feeling as if I were being encouraged, but I didn't dare tell him. I wanted to believe what I had done was a brave and noble thing, but somehow I feared his reaction. I never could impress him with my grades, or my writing. This flag thing would probably upset him. Maybe he, too, would think I was crazy, disrespectful, a "smart-ass" who didn't know his place. I feared that, feared my father saying to me, in a reptile voice, "Let me tell you, you're nothing."

I suited up my G.I. Joe for combat, slipping on his helmet, strapping on his field pack. I fixed the bayonet to his rifle, sticking it in his clutching hands so he seemed ready to fire. "A man's gotta do what a man's gotta do." Was that John Wayne? I don't know who it was, but I did what I had to do, still not telling my father. The following week, in the auditorium, I did it again. This time, everyone noticed. The whole place fell into a weird hush as Mr. Rios screamed at me.

I ended up in my corner again, this time getting a prolonged, pensive stare from the principal before I was made to stare at the wall for two more hours. My mind zoomed past my surroundings. In one strange vision, I saw my crony Edwin climbing up Miss Colon's curvy legs, giving me every detail of what he saw.

"Why?" Miss Colon asked frantically. "This time you don't leave until you tell me why." She was holding me by the arm, masses of kids flying by, happy blurs that faded into the sunlight outside the door.

"Because I'm Puerto Rican, not American," I blurted out in a weary torrent. "That makes sense, don't it?"

"So am I," she said, "but we're in America!" She smiled. "Don't you think you could make some kind of compromise?" She tilted her head to one side and said, "Aw, c'mon," in a little-girl whisper.

"What about standing up for what you believe in? Doesn't that matter? You used to talk to us about Kent State and protesting. You said those kids died because they believed in freedom, right? Well, I feel like them now. I wanna make a stand."

She sighed with evident aggravation. She caressed my hair. For a moment, I thought she was going to kiss me. She was going to say something, but just as her pretty lips parted, I caught Mr. Rios approaching.

"I don't wanna see him," I said, pulling away.

"No, wait," she said gently.

"He's gonna deck me," I said to her.

"No, he's not," Miss Colon said, as if challenging him, her eyes taking him in as he stood beside her.

"No, I'm not," he said. "Listen here. Miss Colon was talking to me about you, and I agree with her." He looked like a nervous little boy in front of the class, making his report. "You have a lot of guts. Still, there are rules here. I'm willing to make a deal with you. You go home and think about this. Tomorrow I'll come see you." I looked at him skeptically, and he added, "to talk."

"I'm not changing my mind," I said. Miss Colon exhaled painfully.

"If you don't, it's out of my hands." He frowned and looked at her. She shook her head, as if she were upset with him.

I re-read the book about Albizu. I didn't sleep a wink that

night. I didn't tell my father a word, even though I almost burst from the effort. At night, alone in my bed, images attacked me. I saw Miss Marti and Mr. Rios debating Albizu Campos. I saw him in a wheelchair with a flag draped over his body like a holy robe. They would not do that to me. They were bound to break me the way Albizu was broken, not by young smiling American troops bearing chocolate bars, but by conniving, double-dealing, self-serving Puerto Rican landowners and their ilk, who dared say they were the future. They spoke of dignity and democracy while teaching Puerto Ricans how to cling to the great coat of that powerful northern neighbor. Puerto Rico, the shining star, the great lap dog of the Caribbean. I saw my father, the Nationalist hero, screaming from his podium, his great oration stirring everyone around him to acts of bravery. There was a shining arrogance in his eyes as he stared out over the sea of faces mouthing his name, a sparkling audacity that invited and incited. There didn't seem to be fear anywhere in him, only the urge to rush to the attack, with his arm band and revolutionary tunic. I stared up at him, transfixed. I stood by the podium, his personal adjutant, while his voice rang through the stadium. "We are not, nor will we ever be, Yankee flag-wavers!" The roar that followed drowned out the whole world.

The following day, I sat in my seat, ignoring Miss Colon as she neatly drew triangles on the board with the help of plastic stencils. She was using colored chalk, her favorite. Edwin, sitting beside me, was beaning girls with spitballs that he fired through his hollowed-out Bic pen. They didn't cry out. They simply enlisted the help of a girl named Gloria who sat a few desks behind him. She very skillfully nailed him with a thick wad of gum. It stayed in his hair until Edwin finally went running to Miss Colon. She used her huge teacher's scissors. I couldn't stand it. They all seemed trapped in a world of trivial things, while I swam in a mire of oppression. I walked through lunch as if in a trance, a prisoner on death row waiting for the heavy steps of his executioners. I watched Edwin lick at his regulation cafeteria ice cream, sandwiched between two sheets of paper. I was once like him, laughing and joking, lining up for a stickball game in the yard without a care. Now it all seemed lost to me, as if my youth had been burned out of me by a book.

Shortly after lunch, Mr. Rios appeared. He talked to Miss Colon for a while by the door as the room filled with a bubbling murmur. Then, he motioned for me. I walked through the sudden silence as if in slow motion.

"Well," he said to me as I stood in the cool hallway, "have you thought about this?"

"Yeah," I said, once again seeing my father on the podium, his voice thundering.

"And?"

"I'm not saluting that flag."

Miss Colon fell against the door jamb as if exhausted. Exasperation passed over Mr. Rios' rodent features.

"I thought you said you'd think about it," he thundered.

"I did. I decided I was right."

"*You* were right?" Mr. Rios was losing his patience. I stood calmly by the wall.

"I told you," Miss Colon whispered to him.

"Listen," he said, ignoring her, "have you heard of the story of the man who had no country?"

I stared at him.

"Well? Have you?"

"No," I answered sharply; his mouse eyes almost crossed with anger at my insolence. "Some stupid fairy tale ain't gonna change my mind anyway. You're treating me like I'm stupid, and I'm not."

"Stop acting like you're some mature adult! You're not. You're just a puny kid."

"Well, this puny kid still ain't gonna salute that flag."

"You were born here," Miss Colon interjected patiently,

trying to calm us both down. "Don't you think you at least owe this country some respect? At least?"

"I had no choice about where I was born. And I was born poor."

"So what?" Mr. Rios screamed. "There are plenty of poor people who respect the flag. Look around you, dammit! You see any rich people here? I'm not rich either!" He tugged on my arm. "This country takes care of Puerto Rico, don't you see that? Don't you know anything about politics?"

"Do you know what imperialism is?"

The two of them stared at each other.

"I don't believe you," Mr. Rios murmured.

"Puerto Rico is a colony," I said, a direct quote of Albizu's. "Why I gotta respect that?"

Miss Colon stared at me with her black saucer eyes, a slight trace of a grin on her features. It encouraged me. In that one moment, I felt strong, suddenly aware of my territory and my knowledge of it. I no longer felt like a boy but some kind of soldier, my bayonet stained with the blood of my enemy. There was no doubt about it. Mr. Rios was the enemy, and I was beating him. The more he tried to treat me like a child, the more defiant I became, his arguments falling like twisted armor. He shut his eyes and pressed the bridge of his nose.

"You're out of my hands," he said.

Miss Colon gave me a sympathetic look before she vanished into the classroom again. Mr. Rios led me downstairs without another word. His face was completely red. I expected to be put in my corner again, but this time Mr. Rios sat me down in the leather chair facing the principal's desk. He stepped outside, and I could hear the familiar clack-clack that could only belong to Miss Marti's reptile legs. They were talking in whispers. I expected her to come in at any moment, but the principal walked in instead. He came in quietly, holding a folder in his hand. His soft brown eyes and beard made him look compassionate, rounded cheeks making him seem friendly. His desk plate solemnly stated: Mr. Sepulveda, PRINCIPAL. He fell into his seat rather unceremoniously, opened the folder, and crossed his hands over it.

"Well, well, well," he said softly, with a tight-lipped grin. "You've created quite a stir, young man." It sounded to me like movie dialogue.

"First of all, let me say I know about you. I have your record right here, and everything in it is very impressive. Good grades, good attitude, your teachers all have adored you. But I wonder if maybe this hasn't gone to your head? Because everything is going for you here, and you're throwing it all away."

He leaned back in his chair. "We have rules, all of us. There are rules even I must live by. People who don't obey them get disciplined. This will all go on your record, and a pretty good one you've had so far. Why ruin it? This'll follow you for life. You don't want to end up losing a good job opportunity in government or in the armed forces because as a child you indulged your imagination and refused to salute the flag? I know you can't see how childish it all is now, but you must see it, and because you're smarter than most, I'll put it to you in terms you can understand.

"To me, this is a simple case of rules and regulations. Someday, when you're older," he paused here, obviously amused by the sound of his own voice, "you can go to rallies and protest marches and express your rebellious tendencies. But right now, you are a minor, under this school's jurisdiction. That means you follow the rules, no matter what you think of them. You can join the Young Lords later."

I stared at him, overwhelmed by his huge desk, his pompous mannerisms and status. I would agree with everything, I felt, and then, the following week, I would refuse once again. I would fight him then, even though he hadn't tried to humiliate me or insult my intelligence. I would continue to fight, until I...

"I spoke with your father," he said.

The Boy Without a Flag

I started. "My father?" Vague images and hopes flared through my mind briefly.

"Yes. I talked to him at length. He agrees with me that you've gotten a little out of hand."

My blood reversed direction in my veins. I felt as if I were going to collapse. I gripped the armrests of my chair. There was no way this could be true, no way at all! My father was supposed to ride in like the cavalry, not abandon me to the enemy! I pressed my wet eyes with my fingers. It must be a lie.

"He blames himself for your behavior," the principal said. "He's already here," Mr. Rios said from the door, motioning my father inside. Seeing him wearing his black weather-beaten trench coat almost asphyxiated me. His eyes, red with concern, pulled at me painfully. He came over to me first while the principal rose slightly, as if greeting a head of state. There was a look of dread on my father's face as he looked at me. He seemed utterly lost.

"Mr. Sepulveda," he said, "I never thought a thing like this could happen. My wife and I try to bring him up right. We encourage him to read and write and everything. But you know, this is a shock."

"It's not that terrible, Mr. Rodriguez. You've done very well with him, he's an intelligent boy. He just needs to learn how important obedience is."

"Yes," my father said, turning to me, "yes, you have to obey the rules. You can't do this. It's wrong." He looked at me grimly, as if working on a math problem. One of his hands caressed my head.

There were more words, in Spanish now, but I didn't hear them. I felt like I was falling down a hole. My father, my creator, renouncing his creation, repentant. Not an ounce of him seemed prepared to stand up for me, to shield me from attack. My tears made all the faces around me melt.

"So you see," the principal said to me as I rose, my father

clutching me to him, "if you ever do this again, you will be hurting your father as well as yourself."

I hated myself. I wiped at my face desperately, trying not to make a spectacle of myself. I was just a kid, a tiny kid. Who in the hell did I think I was? I'd have to wait until I was older, like my father, in order to have "convictions."

"I don't want to see you in here again, okay?" the principal said sternly. I nodded dumbly, my father's arm around me as he escorted me through the front office to the door that led to the hallway, where a multitude of children's voices echoed up and down its length like tolling bells.

"Are you crazy?" my father half-whispered to me in Spanish as we stood there. "Do you know how embarrassing this all is? I didn't think you were this stupid. Don't you know anything about dignity, about respect? How could you make a spectacle of yourself? Now you make us all look stupid."

He quieted down as Mr. Rios came over to take me back to class. My father gave me a squeeze and told me he'd see me at home. Then, I walked with a somber Mr. Rios, who oddly wrapped an arm around me all the way back to the classroom.

"Here you go," he said softly as I entered the classroom, and everything fell quiet. I stepped in and walked to my seat without looking at anyone. My cheeks were still damp, my eyes red. I looked like I had been tortured. Edwin stared at me, then he pressed my hand under the table.

"I thought you were dead," he whispered.

Miss Colon threw me worried glances all through the remainder of the class. I wasn't paying attention. I took out my notebook, but my strength ebbed away. I just put my head on the desk and shut my eyes, reliving my father's betrayal. If what I did was so bad, why did I feel more ashamed of him than I did of myself? His words, once so rich and vibrant, now fell to the floor, leaves from a dead tree.

At the end of the class, Miss Colon ordered me to stay after school. She got Mr. Rios to take the class down along

The Boy Without a Flag

with his, and she stayed with me in the darkened room. She shut the door on all the exuberant hallway noise and sat down on Edwin's desk, beside me, her black pumps on his seat.

"Are you okay?" she asked softly, grasping my arm. I told her everything, especially about my father's betrayal. I thought he would be the cavalry, but he was just a coward.

"Tss. Don't be so hard on your father," she said. "He's only trying to do what's best for you."

"And how's this the best for me?" I asked, my voice growing hoarse with hurt.

"I know it's hard for you to understand, but he really was trying to take care of you."

I stared at the blackboard.

"He doesn't understand me," I said, wiping my eyes.

"You'll forget," she whispered.

"No, I won't. I'll remember every time I see that flag. I'll see it and think, 'My father doesn't understand me.'"

Miss Colon sighed deeply. Her fingers were warm on my head, stroking my hair. She gave me a kiss on the cheek. She walked me downstairs, pausing by the doorway. Scores of screaming, laughing kids brushed past us.

"If it's any consolation, I'm on your side," she said, squeezing my arm. I smiled at her, warmth spreading through me. "Go home and listen to the Beatles," she added with a grin.

I stepped out into the sunshine, came down the white stone steps, and stood on the sidewalk. I stared at the towering school building, white and perfect in the sun, indomitable. Across the street, the dingy row of tattered uneven tenements where I lived. I thought of my father. Her words made me feel sorry for him, but I felt sorrier for myself. I couldn't understand back then about a father's love and what a father might give to insure his son safe transit. He had already navigated treacherous waters and now couldn't have me rock the boat. I still had to learn that he had made peace with The Enemy, that The Enemy was already in us. Like the flag I must salute, we were inseparable, yet his compromise made me feel ashamed and defeated. Then I knew I had to find my own peace, away from the bondage of obedience. I had to accept that flag, and my father, someone I would love forever, even if at times to my young, feeble mind he seemed a little imperfect.

NO MORE WAR GAMES

— To Evelyn

Nilsa was standing skillfully balanced on the rubble in her plastic sandals. Her dumb mother had wanted to buy her a pair of sneakers again, but Nilsa had said nah; she was almost twelve, and she wanted those red plastic sandals. She had to start thinking about dressing like a young woman. That's what her friend Cha-Cha told her. Lately it was the only thing Cha-Cha would talk about. So Nilsa got her sandals. They were adorable, she thought, but they weren't really made to walk on rubble, so she tried to step on only the biggest bricks that jutted out from the yard gravel.

"I think they across the streed," Maria said, dropping a stick. She was searching for something heavier, her tiny eyes slitted like dash marks.

"Yeah, I know that, stupid ass," Nilsa said back with a touch of contempt, her eyes avoiding the tiny figure that hopped and skipped at her side. She tried to distract herself with the long lines of abandoned buildings huddling under the purple sky, but they offered no relief. Her empty gaze fell on Maria again. With mounting irritation, Nilsa noticed her picking up another stick. "Don't grab a stick," Nilsa scolded angrily, "grab a rock. Cause you can't throw a rock good, much less a stick!" "I can throw a stick goo'." Maria glared. "Better'n you." Nilsa stared back, hardly singed, wondering if she had sounded that stupid when she had been nine. About three years ago, she had been hopping from brick to brick, murmuring to herself, just like Maria, every day a new song or color. Now, she bit her lip bitterly and asked herself why she was here, the staleness choking her. She turned from the little ogre, who was still glaring. "Oh, come on, stupid, before we lose um." Her voice was weary and resigned.

She crossed Fox Street, the much smaller Maria tailing her carrying a brick. They were entering the other lot when Nilsa turned, almost striking Maria.

"Gah, you so stupid!" Nilsa yelled. "How you gonna throw that brick? You can't even liff it!" She knocked the large brick out of her hands as Maria began to whine. The brick landed in a clump of weeds with a muffled thump. Nilsa found a smaller rock buried in the soft ground. "Gah, I gotta do everythin." She handed it to her.

"I don't like this rock," Maria protested.

"Hey, juss take it, take it an throw it."

"But it's too liddo!" she whined.

"Look, you wanna eat it?" Nilsa stuck it in her face.

"Nah, I'm not hungry now," Maria giggled, a grimy hand covering her mouth.

Oh, why am I here, why am I wasting my time? I should just jet, thought Nilsa, but she fought the feelings. She looked away from the tiny Maria, walking faster, like she wanted to lose her. She could still hear her, laughing, humming, singing, mouthing nonsense words in a loud murmur that made Nilsa feel like smacking her. "Cut it out," she said, like a staff sergeant, making Maria freeze in her tracks.

They entered the heart of the empty yard, brimming with shattered glass and the odor of raw decay. Like the other lots in the area, this desert of garbage teemed with half-demolished tenements and mountains of bricks, the lot peppered with swaying lanes of tall grass that defiantly cut through the filth, growing wild and uncut. Tiny paths sliced through the walls of gently undulating leaves. Clumps of bushes grew against a rusted chain-link fence that, ruptured and severed from its posts, lay over a part of the cement sidewalk like a carpet. In the middle of the field, on a patch of cement, stood two abandoned buildings, protected by the hulk of a stripped Ford. The car was covered by shards that clung to its faded blue chassis like clotted blood.

As they walked past the naked chain-link posts, Nilsa could hardly hold back her urge to smack Maria, who was skipping and squealing like a piglet. Gah! Where was all this bitterness coming from? She couldn't understand it. She had always been happy here. It had always been fun to hang out in yards, explore gutted buildings, play war games. Fun when Patchi, José, and Eddie built their private NO GIRLS ALLOWED clubhouse on the lot across the street. She, Maria, and Cha-Cha had ambushed them, knocking the tin-board walls in and running off, the boys in hot pursuit.

Now it was different. This week, she would be twelve. Cha-Cha had turned twelve just last week. (Their birthdays were a week apart, as all good girlfriends' birthdays should be.) Nilsa noticed the changes right away. For starters, Cha-Cha hadn't come to the yard all week. She started seeing those older boys from as far away as Jackson Avenue. She painted her nails. Dark red. The day before, Nilsa had gone to her house and, sitting on her puffy quilt, had asked her to come out to the yard to play. Cha-Cha had smirked, staring at herself in the mirror. She tried on a different kind of lip gloss. "Hey," she said, her face brightening. "Cherry! It tastes like cherry!" She leaned over on the bed and passed the gloss stick over Nilsa's lips. "Now lick ya lips," Cha-Cha had commanded. Nilsa passed her tongue over her lips. "Yeah, cherry," she said, faking it. "Adorable." (She used this, her current favorite word, having been introduced to it in school by Miss Flores, the knot-haired acne-lady who, at least, had very pretty legs and had made this, among three others, the "word of the week.") "Really," she added, unconvincingly. "So, you comin to the lot or not?"

"No," Cha-Cha said. "I'll juss get myself all dirty. I don't wanna get dirty."

"You can be careful," Nilsa said, knowing instantly that she sounded stupid.

"Yeah, right. I got better things t' do than get all dirty in that gawdamn gawbetch."

"Gah, donchu like to have fun no more?" Nilsa tried to hide the hurt in her voice, rising from the bed.

"Yeah, I like to have fun!" Cha-Cha yelled. "Don't be such a stupid ass. I like to have fun, yeah, but wha chu talkin about," she paused to smirk, "thass kid stuff."

Kid stuff.

Nilsa picked up a beer bottle and shattered it against one of the posts. The shattering sound was real sweet, the sting on her hand pleasant. Adorable almost.

"Ohhhh...yuh bleedin, look!" Maria covered her mouth.

"It's nothin. Gah, shut up! Go on, walk aheada me. You want they should ambush us togetha, or what?" She gave her a shove.

Damn! Cha-Cha is twelve, and she's changed. They had always been together, in school, on the street, screaming in rancid stairwells, their running steps thumping like war drums. They'd sit like generals and plan war games against the boys, Cha-Cha chasing them across lots and school yards in her little blue shorts, the seam on one leg slightly longer than the other one (you really couldn't notice it, but once

The Boy Without a Flag

you're somebody's best friend, you can see these things). She used to tie her long black hair in a ponytail and pretend she was an Indian savage, howling and stamping, throwing rocks and cans. She'd call an attack, and they'd surge forward across the yard towards the madly tottering clubhouse, making the boys run for cover under the barrage of stones. Then Cha-Cha would tease them out of their holes and relish the chase as the boys counterattacked, making the girls fall back behind the long ridge of rubble that surrounded the yard. Cha-Cha would climb on it, prancing back and forth like a belly dancer. "Ah, c'mon, yuh juss a buncha faggits! We wup yuh ass, man!"

"Yeah?" Patchi would yell from the clubhouse. "You come an try that again. You'll see who's a faggit." His tanned face and curly hair would pop up from behind a tin board. "Juss try it!"

Then Cha-Cha turned twelve. Suddenly she didn't want to go to the yard anymore. She didn't want to get dirty, didn't want to play war games. She started going to the Willis Avenue Roller Rink with Papo Delgado from Tinton Avenue, a tall skinny chump who always wore his $70 Pumas unlaced and kept one leg of his pants higher than the other. Nilsa couldn't stand him. Cha-Cha started putting on lipstick and blush and purple eye shadow and all kinds of goo she picked up at the corner discount store, where she could be seen before closing time, staring in wonder at the long line of glittering facial products safely tucked inside a plastic display case. Nilsa got to watch her buy the stuff. She sprawled across the bed while Cha-Cha excitedly jabbered into the mirror, playing with her new toys.

"Whacha put that stuff on for?" she asked disapprovingly. She knew why; she had seen the Maybelline commercials too and knew that the goo stuff led to boys. What she really meant to ask was "Whacha wanna get boys for?", but of course she didn't ask that. That would've been worse.

"It's the only way to get guys," Cha-Cha replied, leaning

over the dresser, dabbing on some rouge. "How do I look?" She seemed to ask the mirror.

"Like some clown," Nilsa said bitterly.

"Come on, yuh juss jealous. Jealous cause you don't have a guy."

"I am not!" Nilsa yelled, rising up from the bed, smashing her fists against the bureau, sending scores of lipsticks and fingernail shades tumbling, clacking, rolling. "I'm not. I could get one if I wanted. I juss don't wanna."

"Admit it, girl, thass why yuh mad at me! It's not cause I don't spend time wif you, it's cause you can't join me, cause you don't wanna stop bein a baby an grow up." She combed out her long black hair with angry strokes. "An cause you don't got a guy."

"Thass not it!!" Nilsa screamed. "You changed, I swear! I toldju, I don't want no boyfriend now."

"Why not? Gonna wait til yuh a ol maid?" She chuckled to herself, picking up a strand of feathers with a clip at the end. "God, you gonna be twelve nex week. You gotta start growin up. You can't keep playin war games forever, you know."

"I know." Nilsa shrugged halfheartedly, playing with a lipstick she had picked up off the bureau, watching the pointed pink tip go in and out. But I like it! I like playing war games, she felt like saying, but instead she just shut her mouth tightly so she wouldn't say anything stupid.

"You juss like being a lil girl, right? God." Cha-Cha's face was lined with sarcasm, a hostile derision that made Nilsa feel sick inside. That golden brown skin sprinkled with rouge and powder, eyes shadowed and blackly lined, lips glossy red... was this really her Cha-Cha, the tomboy she had hung with for six years? Now she was different, a monster with sex glands and a clown face, an ugly grown thing. All of this in just one week! "Grow up," the monster voice said, and tears welled up in Nilsa's eyes.

"Look," Cha-Cha said coldly, "when you grow up, juss

The Boy Without a Flag

lemme know. Maybe we can double date." She picked up
her roller skates, the tiny bells on the striped laces jin-
gling merrily.

"I think that guy yuh with is a real jerk," Nilsa said
angrily, pushing past her, out the door before Cha-Cha could
notice the tears.

*I guess I should dress up. I guess my pants should be
tighta. I mean, these shorts are pretty tight, but they're not
sharp. They're little girl shorts, like f gym. Not sexy. I gotta
maybe tell ma to get me some Alessio jeans, they make ya ass
stick up. I gotta paint my nails, even though they look like boy
nails. Red, like Cha-Cha. I could get some lipstick from the
Discount, an then I could saprize Cha-Cha, hang out with huh
like the ol days. We'll be two foxes. Cha-Cha is right, ain't she?
Can't blame huh for not wanting to play war games in huh
Sergios. After all, they'll get dirty. Or ripped.*

She stamped through the grass, flattening it under her
foot. Nothing felt the same anymore. Something about the
yard had been stolen from her. She felt like leaving silly little
Maria by herself.

Suddenly, a rock smacked into the glass shards nearby.
She looked up and saw Eddie and Patchi's faces peering down
at them from a third-floor window. Scores of stones rained
down with tiny thumps. The boys yelled, "Ambush!", swinging
their arms through the air, now throwing heavier rocks,
bricks, and cans.

"Run, Nilsa! It's af rambush!" Maria screamed, running
towards the tall grass. She tossed a rock that hit the building
ineffectually.

Af rambush? Of course! Af rambush! For a moment, she
felt the old excitement flutter through her as she picked up a
jagged chunk of brick and threw it. A sharp stone crashed into
her leg, leaving a white scratch that trailed across her thigh.
The stinging blow angered her. Without thinking, she picked
up a bottle and threw it, hitting the window frame savagely,

sending the two boys down from the sill for shelter inside as the bottle exploded. Glass spattered everywhere and tinkled softly down, with a noise like wind chimes.

Eddie's head stuck up through the window like a cabbage with curly hair. His face showed astonishment.

"We three floors up!" he yelled, looking at her with some admiration. "How she throw that up here?"

"Shut up," Patchi said gruffly. They both vanished, to reappear in a second-floor window with a large glass jug.

"If you throw bottles, we throw bottles!" Eddie yelled defiantly.

"I don't give a damn, faggits," Nilsa said back, her legs apart, hands on hips, almost a replica of the old Cha-Cha. "Go ahead. If you got the guts."

"I got the guts," Eddie said, looking at Patchi, who was keeping out of sight. The glass jug whirled through the air sluggishly and landed in the tall grass without even shattering.

"Stupid ass!" Nilsa yelled, Maria squealing with derision.

"You gotta throw it harder," Patchi told Eddie angrily.

"Throw it? I could hardly liff it."

"Gimme the other one. I'll throw it," Patchi demanded.

"What? Nah man, I thought we were both gonna—" Eddie suddenly fell backwards as a stone smacked him loudly on the forehead.

"Oh shit!" Patchi half-yelled, laughing. He peered over the edge of the sill and ducked just in time to avoid getting hit by another rock. It clattered against the back wall and almost nailed Eddie again on the rebound.

"Thass right, I'll hit you too, faggit," Nilsa yelled, hands on hips as she rocked from foot to foot. (Another Cha-Cha staple.)

"We betta throw that damn bottle," Patchi said, Eddie rubbing his war wound. The two of them picked up the huge water-cooler bottle, yellowish gray water sloshing around inside.

"Prepare to be bombed!" Patchi yelled.

Nilsa did not wait. She called on Maria to follow her as she jumped down the concrete incline quickly, past the stripped Ford, and into the building. "Come on, stupid!"

"Nah, I can't go in there," Maria replied shyly, some fingers in her mouth as she stood by the car. "Junkies."

"Fuck you, then," Nilsa murmured under her breath, jumping onto the ground floor, her sandals crunching glass underneath. The stagnant odor of rotting wood and piss overwhelmed her as she worked her way through the apartment, looking for the way upstairs.

"Ey, where'd she go?" Eddie yelled. Nilsa laughed, hearing his voice muffled through the chipped ceiling, sounding close. "Look. There's the runt. Let's throw it at huh." There was a weird pause. Nilsa went over to a window to see.

There was a great crash. The water-cooler bottle had landed on the car and shattered, spraying Maria with lethal chunks of glistening glass. She screamed, running away as fast as she could down the path that sliced through the wall of tall grass, scared but unscathed.

Nilsa hurried through the apartment, finding the way out into the dank, putrid hallway. She had to step carefully over ugly beams that hung down from the torn walls. She saw something on a landing she could use: a Bacardi bottle, full of murky water. She drained it, spreading her legs far apart so she wouldn't get her sandals wet as the water gurgled out of the bottle and splashed down the stairs.

She crept up the stairs quietly, half-darkness cloaking her, sunlight raining through open apartment doors in slivers. She could hear them laughing. She followed the sound, which led her right to them. The half-open door creaked a little as she slipped in. There were pretty patterns on the peeling wallpaper by the door that reminded her a little of her house. She kept her steps light on the noisy rubble, a strange feline feeling creeping through her. She felt like some animal of prey, maybe a hero soldier in a war movie, only this was better because she was a girl, a lioness, or cheetah-ess, or whatever. A pleasurable tremor coursed through her as she cautiously approached her prey, feeling devious, sneaky, sexy...

Sexy?

She spotted the two of them from her end of the hall, which led into the living room. There were bits of glass sparkling everywhere like miniature lights and a couch with its springs showing through torn fabric like the rib cage on a carcass.

"Hey, they musta retreated," Eddie said proudly as the two leaned out the window. "Looks like we won."

"Yeah, I guess we won, cause they—"

Nilsa suddenly shrieked. It was an ear-piercing sirenlike scream that made them both jump into the air. Before they could recover, she threw her Bacardi bottle. It shattered majestically against a nearby wall, glass bursting like crystal, reverberating over and over loudly, tinkling forever as the twinkling shards rained down on the stunned pair. She screamed again, and the walls rattled and shook in their heads.

"Oh shit!" Eddie yelled, his shoulder-length black hair obstructing his vision, making him trip over debris as he raced off into the next room. She heard him jump onto the fire escape, while Patchi was still stumbling blindly after having tripped.

"Come on, Patch! Quick! Before she makes you a prisona!" The frantic steps Eddie took down the fire-escape ladder made it rumble.

Patchi was about to whirl around and make his escape too, but Nilsa grabbed his wrist forcefully and turned his arm around.

"Ow, gawdammit!" he yelled in frustration and surprise. "Hey! Yuh gonna break my arm!"

"I will if you don't do what I say," Nilsa said proudly. "Yuh my prisona." She tugged on his arm a little and felt something twisting around in her chest that made her feel giddy and powerful. She tightened her grip on him. "Come ova here, by the wall."

She pulled him—he had no choice. He could hear Eddie, outside, calling to him. What a bastid, he thought bitterly. Insteada standin around outside yellin, he should come in an liberate me. It was the bottle. The bottle scared the gawdamn shit outta him. He's probably down there now, scrapin it off his pants. Bastid.

"Now what?" he asked. "Hey, easy wid the arm."

"Shut up!" Nilsa commanded. He struggled suddenly and yelled from the pain as she twisted his arm fiercely. She kept expecting something to crack. When he stopped wriggling, she loosened her grip. "Okay, whachu want?" Patchi asked, wincing.

She stared at the back of his head, stepping close to examine his profile. He looked at her anxiously. She felt powerful, in command for once! He was her prisoner. She could make him do anything she wanted, anything! He was helpless. She wanted to prolong the moment, maybe for a week or two, just to keep that joyful spinning in her head going.

Where was Cha-Cha now? Here was Nilsa, in control, confident in her abilities. She could have anything she wanted, even boys. She'd be a great pioneer woman who could play war games and rip her jeans up and still go out with boys and look beautiful. Cha-Cha was just too limited.

She stared at Patchi with what she felt were the eyes of a mature twelve-year-old woman. Once she turned those eyes on him, she could feel him sweat. His tan was like a coat of grime, his curly hair soft and shiny and stuck to his head. His brown eyes had strange lights living in them. She might've preferred it to be Eddie, with his wild Indian looks and his thick long hair, but she'd settle. He couldn't refuse her. She was in command. She knew what she wanted him to do.

"Kiss me," she said.

"What?" Patchi squirmed under her serious expression,

turning red to the roots of his hair. "Yuh nuts—" He squirmed but stopped, the rest of his words caught in his throat as she twisted the arm again. "Youch, okay, okay, easy, easy...yuh kiddin, right?"

"Nah. I mean it. Kiss me. Right on the lips. Yuh my prisona. You gotta do what I say."

He stared at her. "Yuh serious."

She nodded, straightening his arm, her face softening expectantly. She gripped his hand securely. "Whass the matter? You ain't neva kiss a girl before?"

He blushed again. "Sure I kiss a girl before!" he said indignantly. "It's juss a strange thing t' do."

"To kiss a girl, thass strange?"

"Nah, I mean...you know what I mean." He stared at the ceiling, exasperated.

"Well, come on, do it," she said, tightening her grip on his arm with both hands now, "or I'll break it."

"On the cheek, you said?"

"Uh-uh. On the lips." She pointed to her lips with a finger, grinning. "You neva kissed a girl before!"

"I have too! I'm juss nerviss!" Patch replied angrily. "God, you put me on the spot, I swear!"

"Maybe you don't think I'm pretty enough. Is that why?" Nilsa tightened her grip. "Maybe if it had been Cha-Cha, an not me, maybe you woulda kissed huh, right? You woulda been all over huh, right?" She twisted his arm viciously, anger coursing through her. "Thass why! Cause I'm not Cha-Cha. You damn bastid!" She was going to kill him. She couldn't have him, but neither could Cha-Cha. Her mother and her little brother could come visit her weekends at Riker's Island...

"Nah, thass not why, stop!! It hurts, I neva said I din't like you, stop!!" Patchi's voice grew frantic when he felt the pressure increasing. He closed his eyes and awaited the snap, but suddenly she stopped twisting his arm. Standing before him, she held on to his throbbing arm and stared.

The Boy Without a Flag

"Well?" she asked.

"Well what?" He was stalling.

"Do you think I'm pretty, or donchu?" She squeezed his arm with emphasis. Dammit, she was gonna get the answer she wanted, or else...

He paused, his features reddening again. "Yuh all right," he said quietly, looking away from her face. It had been more than he wanted to say and less than she wanted to hear.

Something crumbled into tiny bits inside of her. The disappointment of it all was too much, too soon. Cha-Cha was right about her. She was just a creepy twelve-year-old who should grow up, who couldn't even force a boy to kiss her, a prisoner at that! If he had only done it, it would've been okay, okay to befriend the empty lots and mountains of rubble, to fight and chase and claw and battle, to play war games and still be grown up and get boyfriends, but it didn't happen that way. Now Nilsa was shattered and embarrassed, more embarrassed than she had been in her entire life. She let go of his hand, her face stinging painfully.

"Forget it," she said feebly. "Forget I said anything."

Patchi looked at her, then at the fire escape across the room. He took two steps, then froze, trying to think of the right thing to do, his arm still throbbing. He felt stupid for having been taken prisoner. He was seriously considering whacking her around a bit, just to sort of preserve his manhood, but when he looked at her, she looked so broken and delicate that he decided just to jet, leaping out onto the fire escape.

Nilsa watched him go, listening to the thumping of his steps on the tired metal. Maria was calling for her. She walked over to the window and watched her, a tiny figure dwarfed by the tall grass that swayed and swished around her gently.

Nilsa felt different. The whole place looked and smelled different. Something was gone forever, but Nilsa didn't know what that was. All she knew was that this running around in empty lots was no longer enough.

A strange fatigue overwhelmed her as she climbed out on the fire escape. Nilsa watched Maria dance in the grass, tiny arms waving happily, her voice a rubber-toy squeak carried by the warm breezes.

Nilsa descended.

She knew that tomorrow she would get those tight French jeans. She would talk to Cha-Cha about painting her nails and getting the right color lipstick. She would style her hair and wear gaily-colored feathers in strands of silky interwoven braid.

And there would be no more war games.

BABIES

It was good fucken shit, not that second-rate stuff. It was
really good shit, the kind you pay a lot for, so I stared at Smiley
for a while cause I got real curious bout whea the money
came from.

"What," he said, lookin at me while he rolled anotha joint.

"Whea you get the money, macho?" I axed him, an he
started backin up into the riot gate we were standin in front of.

"Aw, c'mon, don't start."

"Me start?" I yelled, real loud, cause I knew it bugged
him whenever I did that on the street an everyone knew our
problems. "I'm not startin nothin, I juss wanna know whea
you got the money, whachu been husslin."

"It wasn't no hussle, *muñeca*, juss chill out."

"Yeah, yeah, I heard that before, man. If the fucken cops
come snoopin around the house for yuh ass again, Smiley
man, thass it, we're through. I don't wanna fucken hassle with
that no more."

"Shut up an, like, smoke."

I'm serious, Smiley got some real special shit, don't taste like tree bark. We smoked an hung out for a while, then Smiley went to the Super to see bout maybe gettin some work, cause usually Smiley could get somethin to do, like plumbin or puttin up a ceilin someplace, an then we could have money for rent. The goddamn food stamps ran out. Now we're in some serious shit. I din't know before, but when I went upstairs with my friend Sara, I saw the empty book. I'll tell you somethin else we ain't got: food. I checked the frigerator an the bastid's empty, even the light bulb quit on us. It smells all mildewy in thea, an thea's some green shit growin in the egg tray. Clusters of dead roaches float in some dingy water at the bottom. Thea's a half-empty box of Sugar Pops. Dinner.

Check it out, Smiley don't really care bout food anyway. When we first moved in together, he knew I couldn't cook for shit, but he said fuck it, cause he wanted his favorite piece of ass with him. (Thass my sentimental Smiley!) Thea's no housecleanin either cause thea ain't much of a house, juss a two-room apartment on the fifth floor that came complete with a mattress. (We washed it off first.) We got a small black-and-white TV, a love seat that smells funny an has a paint can for a fourth leg, an a old bureau we grabbed off the street that came with its very own roaches. (For free! Whea else but in America?) Thass all our furniture. We got a gray exercise mat we use like a dinin area on the floor, so when people come to eat they gotta sit on the floor like chinks or those hindoos.

Sara hung out with me for a while until we finished the last joint. She has a radio. It's really her man's, but she carries it around anyway. She played it while we sat by the windows, cause it was spring an the breeze was cool an fresh. Sara is kinda dark, but she's Rican, with long hair. She's gotten a little fat, but then she had a baby bout two weeks ago.

"Whea's the baby anyway?" I axed, thinkin bout that little dark bundle I saw wrapped tightly in blue at Lincoln Hospital when she had it an I went to visit.

"It's around," she said tiredly, not wantin to talk bout it.

"Whea around?"

"I think Madgie's with him outside the bakery. Or maybe I leff him by the liquor store. I dunno." She shrugged like thea was a bug on her shoulder.

"Man, you gotta cut that shit out," I said, without too much conviction. "Yuh a motha now," I added, feelin it was the right thing to say an shit. "You gotta be responsible an take care of your baby."

"I know," she said loud, forehead all pruned up. "I know that! What, chu think I don't know? You think I treat my baby mean? He hangs out with me alla time! Alla time, dammit, he's thea, remindin me!" She lay back on our dinin mat. "Shit. Tell me I don't care bout my kid. I bet if you had a kid, you do better?"

I din't say nothin cause I knew she was all crotchety bout that kid. This always happens with her, so, like always, I juss let her blow all her steam out. You could tell it was botherin her. Her man (not the one with the radio, he's the new man), the father of the kid, at first seemed hip to the idea of a boy, but then he got real pissed off. One night, they were outside the liquor store an it was bout midnight. They were both drinkin, an they got in a fight. He wanted to know what right she had to fuck up his life. All he knows how to do is drink an stan around, he ain't got time for no babies, so what she come with this shit now for? She threw a half-empty bottle of Smirnoff at him, which really upset some of the otha winos nearby cause it was such a waste of good drinkin stuff. She got all teary an stood out in the middle of the street with the baby carriage.

"Fuck you!" she screamed, all hoarse. "I don't give a fuck!" An swoosh, a car passed bout three inches from the baby carriage.

"I hope you get kill, bitch!" he screamed back.

A big bus appeared, one of those new air condition ones from Japan that look like bullets. It started honkin. She swung the baby carriage at it. Thass when I stepped in. I had been waitin for Smiley an saw the whole thing. I dragged her off the street to her house whea I fixed her a drink. (Her apartment, by the way, is worse than ours. At least ours has a ceilin over the bathroom.) The baby was cryin like somebody stepped on it. "Put this over his face an he'll shut up," she said, handin me a blanket. "It always works."

I took him into the bathroom, the only otha room in that dump thass private, an I shut the door on him so his cryin sounded far-off an echoey.

"I'm so fucked up!" she wailed. "I lost my man, an here I am stuck with that...that...ohhhh, fuck that bastid! Mothafucka, iss all his fault! To hell with him! Who needs him? You think I need him to bring up the baby? I'll bring it up all on my own, who needs him? That prick. He better gimme money, ain't no way he's gonna walk out on me an not gimme money, I don't care if we ain't married, he still has to gimme money, that bastid..."

"If you don't stop screamin, the baby ain't never gonna shut up an sleep," I said.

Her eyes got all wild. "Din't I tell you," she screamed, "to put a blanket over it? Put a blanket over the baby's head an it'll shut up!"

So much for the memory. She was lyin on the dinin mat like a corpse, her eyes cuttin holes in the ceilin. Everything was quiet now. When the joint finished, she tuned the radio to some house music.

"So whachu name the baby?" I axed, now that she had calmed down.

"Baby," she said. "It's called Baby."

I grimaced. "Thass stupid."

"Fuck you, juss whachu know bout babies?"

Okay: I know that I got leff in a carriage in the hot sun when I was a baby, my older brotha told me. He said my motha got drunk an forgot whea I was, an I hadda go to the hospital. I remember when I was three, my motha was with this man. She got drunk an put a hankie over my eyes so I couldn't see, then the two of them spun me around an around. They sped off in his Camaro, strandin me on Randall's Island for a long time. I got lost an walked around an cried a river, until cops saw me an took my hands an told me stories. They showed up in the Camaro an felt all embarrassed. A big Irish cop with a thick mustache got real mad. He noticed they were both stoned an gave them tickets. When we got home, my motha beat the livin shit outta me. "It was juss a game," she howled, "You din't have to go fuck it up."

"I don't know," I said to Sara. "I'm juss fucked up." I got up, away from her. I din't wanna talk bout babies no more. I went to my favorite drawer in the bureau an got my stuff. Sara watched. She liked to watch me shoot up, though she never did H cause she said she din't wanna die. She juss liked to watch an ax stupid questions like if it was school an I was her tutor. I took out my kit but let it lie for a while cause I was still buzzin from the joint.

I hate it when people say I'm a junkie an shit cause it's really not true. I know I got it all under control, an plus I know I can stop anytime I want. (I did once, for three whole days, an then since I knew I could take it or leave it, I took it, cause I mean, what else is thea? Why shouldn't I feel sweet?) Some Hispanos been axin me whea I picked up such a habit, cause around 149th thea ain't no sixteen-year-old girls on H. The fack is, I used to hang out in the village with this funky guy named Matt who used to do crazy shit like steal cars for a day juss to ride around. I met him through a friend in junior high. Me and him used to hang out a lot in that park with the big white arch thing whea he used to deal H to all the junkies who hung thea. I axed him what it was like to take H, cause I seen him sniffin it, an he gimme a book to read: *Christiane F.* I read like four pages an said enough of this shit, I hate books.

He got mad an said I should learn somethin, but I wouldn't go near it again, so he said fuck it, I should learn the hard way then. He shot me full of H. I first felt like I was gonna throw up on him, my stomach was dribblin around an my head felt like it was separatin from my body. I got real nervous until Matt told me to relax an not be uptight, an then I started feelin real good. The next day he shot me up again an made a joke bout that bein my last free sample. When that freeze hit me, I was on cloud nine, ten, eleven. I was free of everythin that bugged my head out, like my motha, who was out fucken like a dog in heat, or my bad grades in school, or my older brotha, who one day disappeared without even a fucken poof leavin only a pair of Pro Keds on the kitchen table as a good-bye. Nah, I wasn't thinkin bout nothin at all, juss gettin more sweet H an takin more trips into that sweet nothin land.

I hadda keep shootin after that. One time I bought some real bad shit from some guy I din't know, a fucken Latin dude, an it was awful. I felt like if bugs were crawlin all over an I couldn't stop scratchin. That was the only time I ever got fucked up. That was a year ago that I turned on, I mean, an since then, I haven't gotten the sunken face or the bags under the eyes or the circles neither. I look great. In fack, guys keep axin me out all the time, but I got Smiley, so I say nah. I'd only be like my motha if I said yeah.

Smiley's two years older than me. He's tall an sleek, with a sorta beard that feels nice. He smokes pot like a stove. He dropped out of high school to work in a car shop on Bruckner Boulevard. He lived in whass now our place with two otha dudes cause his father hated him an his motha din't really care bout nothin much. His father used to beat her around like a Ping-Pong. Smiley got sick of it, so one day, durin one of his father's drunken freak-outs, Smiley took a kitchen knife an stabbed him. Yeah, Smiley stuck him, an they threw him in Riker's Island for six months. I think thass one of the most heroic things I ever heard of in my life, which is why I really love him, cause he's so sweet an courageous. He met me one day cause one of his roomies, a thin kid with a bushy head an a face used to stompins, brought him to school to hang out, an he met me in the cafeteria. We started seein each otha an got it on. Six months ago, he kicked out his roomies for bein slobs, an he axed me to move in. You betcha ass I did. I leff my nympho bottle-sucking motha on Cypress Avenue with her roomful of men doin rotatin shifts. She din't miss me.

For a little while, thea were fluffy clouds an flowers an what they call "romance" on TV. I should end that whole story with one a those happy-ever-after things like in all great lit, but thea's always trouble. Last summer, the cops busted him twice cause he lost his job an started doin some husslin. Once they caught him with stolen goods, the otha time he got fingered in a muggin. I tried to get him to stop, but then he has to get his smoke, an I need my H; I get real cranky without it.

My buzz faded out, so I lit my juice an shot up quick, cause Sara was gettin loud. (She always does when she gets high, always sayin the stupidest shit as loud as she can.) I juss floated away an only came back to the room years later when she mentioned Diana.

Check it out, Diana is this sixteen-year-old girl who's really preggoes, like out to here. I don't know how many fucken months gone by. She's younga lookin than I am an has a real pretty complexion, like an Ivory girl, skin dark an smooth, eyes bright, tiny red lips that pout, a nice narrow waist. The first time I seen her, when she moved in with her motha an sister, I said, this one won't last. She din't. She got fucked fast enough by this guy everybody knows, named Freddie, who thinks he's all bad an acts like a beat boy. Now she's real big, an he's nowhere in sight.

"I know her motha," Sara was sayin, walkin around real fast. "I talk to her alla time, you know, she like, talks to me, knows I'm a motha too. She's a real slick lady, no shit. Works in Lerner's, that store? The one on Third Avenue, no shit, she sells dresses." She laughed hysterically for some fucken reason. I told you, she gets this way when she's on smoke.

"An like, she's a real decent, upstandin woman, she don't be hangin out with all these scums an shit heads. She got it all together. She really care bout her two girls, which is why issa shame bout Diana. An Marissa be fourteen nex month. Hope it don't happen to her!"

Yeah, Marissa, fourteen, wears black boots an skintight pants an waist cords an glossy lipstick an two huge plastic heart earrings. She's next. Nah, I don't think it's good for a growin girl to have a motha who works at Lerner's.

"Though I seen her yesterday, she was wearin a miniskirt with those…those wild panny hoses an shit with the designs on them? Shit, man. Her motha dresses her real good. She's really a motha, you know." She leaned real close to me. "She's tryin to get Diana to get a abortion."

"It's too late," I said, knowin Diana was too far gone for one.

"Yeah, but she knows somebody who'll still do it, an cheap too. I told you, girl, I talk to her, she confide in me an shit! I tole her it was the right thing to do. Babies can be the death, man. I tole her I shoulda aborted mines. You know? I axed her if she wanted my baby, but she said nah."

I started laughin. That was really wild!

"I'm serious, *muñeca*, I really meant it, cause I know she's a good motha."

"An she said no?"

"Yeah."

"You really give yuh baby away to somebody if they take him?"

"Sure, why not?" she said, gettin up, as if I insulted her or somethin. "She can bring it up good. Give it a good home, an toys, an money, an shit." She wasn't facin me. "I don't wanna talk bout this no more."

"Okay," I said, feelin like I did somethin wrong. "You

want some Sugar Pops?" I brought the box over from the
fridge an dug deep into it, poppin the stuff into my mouth.
"Nah, I gotta go," she said, an poof, a kiss on the cheek an
she was out the door, with the fucken radio too.

Talkin to Sara bout babies made me feel funny inside.
It's like, I don't know, I think I could be a great motha sometimes, but then I think maybe I'm too fucked up to even take
care of myself, an I don't know enough bout things an life, an
maybe I'll juss fuck up the kid. Those otha times, when I think
I could really swing it an be a good motha are kinda painful
cause it gets like an itch, an it makes me wanna swell up right
away. I guess cause I was thinkin bout it so much, an cause I
was high on H, when Smiley came in late at night, I axed him
bout babies.

"What about um?" he axed back, rollin a joint as he sat
on our dinin mat.

"Do you ever think of havin one? One for us?" The
thought made me all crazy. I hugged him, like I had a billion
tiny worms dancin in my veins. He pushed me away, got
real serious.

"You not pregnint," he said, angry. "You pregnint?"

"No, Smiley, I—"

"You better not get fucken pregnint, or I'm out the fucken
door. You see that door?" he yelled, pointin to it. "I be out of it
if you get pregnint. I ain't supportin no fucken baby. Thass
that. No way. Be bad enough supportin me an you." He got up,
lickin his joint shut. "You got enough H?" he axed before he
went into the "bedroom."

"Yeah," I said, feeling like somethin got taken out. He saw
my spression an kinda felt bad, so he came over an kissed me
an picked me up like some baby an planted me in bed an
kissed me again. "Now, we don't want no babies, okay?"

"Okay," I said.

An then we fucked.

❖ ❖ ❖ ❖

The next night, I was sittin on the stoop with Diana. It wasn't like I planned it or nothin, it's juss Smiley wasn't home, an I decided to wait for him outside. I had been in the fucken apartment all day long, throwin up, mostly. Maybe it was the smoke an the H? I told Millie bout it, an she laughed an said, "Uh-oh," but the bitch vanished before I could get the story out of her.

Anyway, I was gonna hang out for a while an went downstairs. Thass when I heard cryin, soft cryin an sniffin. I looked down the hallway an saw somebody down by the otha stairwell that goes to the otha side of the buildin. It was juss the top of a head behind the handrail whea everybody puts their garbage. I walked right over, cause I'm a curious bitch, an saw it was Diana in a cute blue maternity thing that said BABY an had a arrow pointin to her belly. She heard me sneakin up an got all self-conscious. We weren't really close or nothin, juss talked once or twice, so I started yappin a whole lot, first bout the smell of the hallway, then garbage. I told her my top ten worst insects list (she cracked up), an then finally I got to ax. "So how come yuh down here cryin?"

Diana kinda sighed an rearranged her long hair with a toss of her head. She wiped at her face clumsily. "My motha an I had anotha fight about the baby."

"She still wancha get rid of it?"

"Yeah. She knows I'm seven months," her voice cracked, "but she don't care. She says she's gonna do whass bess for me if she gotta break the law to do it, an she says she'll drag me down if I don't want to. I juss wasn't inna mood for all that shit tonight, so I juss ducked out."

"What bout your man, whea's he?" I tried soundin like a therapist I saw on TV.

"I don't know. Freddie went away. I ain't seen him in six months." She started to cry again, an I gave her a big hug. She was tremblin a little, juss like Sara's baby when I first picked it up from its crib two weeks ago an it looked like a tiny red prune. We walked out to the stoop an sat thea for a while.

"You think your motha's gonna come down an getchu?" I axed.

"I don't know. She'll send Marissa. She expected me to sit thea an hear anotha sermon about what I gotta do, but I'm not gonna, I'm not gonna kill my baby," she said firmly, her voice gettin louder, "because it's mines, an Freddie's, an someday he'll come back, an even if he doesn't, so what? The baby is…a produck of our love for each otha, a part of us, you know? Thea's a part of me in that baby, an if I let her kill it, she'll be killin somethin of mines! I feel it, you know? It moves around in thea. It does bumps an grinds an shit! It's juss waitin to be born. I'm not gonna let her murder my baby!" she yelled, clenching her fists as if she was gonna punch me.

"Don't get so worked up," I said, tryin to calm her down.

"Worked up? Don't get so worked up? You ack like this is somethin trivial, like buyin *lechuga o tomate*! It's not, you know. It's a baby. An it's mines, dammit, mines!"

"An how you gonna bring it up?" I axed, already gettin too involved, but somethin happens to me when I get yelled at. "If you have it, you gonna stay witcha motha?"

"No way. I know a friend who lives near Melrose. She's gettin it ready. In a week, I can go live with her."

"So what? How you gonna bring it up? How you gonna feed it? You got money for that, or is yuh friend also a fucken bank?"

"She's gonna help me til I get on my feet," she said slowly, as if she was tryin to remember lines from a play.

"Yeah? An how you gonna get on yuh feet? You leff school?"

"I'm goin back."

"Takin the baby witcha?"

"Stop it."

"You'll need money for a baby-sitter. Whea's it gonna—"

"Freddie'll help," she said angrily.

"He's halfway to Bermuda by now." I knew that was cruel, but juss who the fuck she think she is yellin at me like that when I try an help?

"Fuck you!" she yelled. "Yuh juss like my motha!"

Thass when Marissa appeared in the doorway, wearin a polka-dot miniskirt with wooden sandals that clacked real loud.

"Ma says to come up," she said, a finger in her mouth.

"I'm not goin up thea. You tell…" The words froze in her mouth, cause juss as she turned to tell Marissa off, she spotted her motha coming down the hall.

"I'm not comin witcha!" Diana screamed, jumpin off the stoop an tryin to run away. This was when her motha put on some speed an grabbed her, pullin her to the stoop again.

"Let her go!" I yelled, tryin to untangle them, but I got an elbow in the face real hard from one of them. They both collapsed on the sidewalk, Diana yellin "I hate'chu!" an throwin punches like a demon. Millie, the daughter of the guy who owns the bodega next door, started yellin for the cops. Diana's motha was hittin back now, an hard, up on her feet while Diana rolled on the ground from the punches, getting soaked from a dribblin hydrant she slid under. Her motha started pullin on her real fierce while screamin bout respect. I thought she'd hurt her or somethin, so I lunged, pullin her away.

"Leave her alone!" I cried.

"Leave her alone?" her motha roared back in my face, her eyes real big. "Leave her alone? With you? She's my daughter! Do you hear? She's my daughter, not yours! My baby! An she's not endin up like you!" Her voice was hoarse, her arms flyin around like pinwheels as she gestured wildly at the crowd (which always forms at the first sign of a free show). "Buncha junkies an shits, you gonna save my daughter from me? I'm savin her from dirt like you!" She grabbed Diana again and started draggin her. "Less see you stop me, *carajo!*" She had completely flipped, her eyes bulgin, her hair a mess, her red blouse all torn up. She kept draggin Diana even though she screamed an swung out at her, her otha arm gettin scratched up from scrapin against the sidewalk. Two guys from the bodega came out an pulled her motha off, because Diana was movin funny, holdin her stomach.

"Oh God!!" she cried, louder than anythin I ever heard in my life. She wriggled an folded into a ball, clutchin her stomach. I bent over her, tryin to unfold her, me an Millie both tried, but we couldn't. When she looked up at me, her face looked horrible, all cracked inside.

"Oh shit, get an ambulance!" I yelled, at nobody an everybody, while Marissa stood frozen to the spot, by the stoop, starin blankly as if watchin TV, absently pullin up on her designer panty hose.

♦ ♦ ♦ ♦

It was a week after that that Sara gave away her baby. She got rid of it somehow, I don't fucken know how, I juss kept seein her without it so I axed her one day, an she juss got this real idiot grin on her face like when she's stoned, an she said, "It's gone," an then she walked away from me with her blarin box, over to her new man by the liquor store, with the gleamin pint of brandy. I juss ran home to my H after that, I juss couldn't deal with it.

I don't know, I don't read much, don't watch news, don't care bout how many got fried in Nicaragua or wherever, but sometimes I get this feelin, an it's not bout politics, cause that guy Matt, who turned me on to H, was a real militant black motha who was always sayin the system hadda be overthrowed, an I think he's still sayin that from his sewer hole somewhere.

Babies 57

I don't got a head for that shit, you know? But this feelin I get. I look out my window an see it all crawlin by, see it all scribbled on Sara's face, stamped on Diana's torn maternity suit. I remember her motha's words, an they all seemed to hit me somewhere. Shit, I even feel it now when I look in the mirror an see the circles under my eyes an the marks on my fucked-up arms: we're in some real serious shit here. It's no place for babies. Not even a good place for dogs.´ I guess I can't pretend I'm alive anymore. Diana's baby was lucky; it died in the incubator. On my seventeenth birthday, I dreamed I was in that incubator, chokin. Smiley woke me up with a cupcake that had a candle on it, yellow flame dancin nervous, like it might go out any second. He remembered.

Smiley noticed I changed a little, cause I wasn't so happy anymore. I juss wanted to take my H an cruise on my run an not botha. He even got mad cause I din't wanna fuck so much no more. I din't tell him I was pregnint, not even after four weeks passed.

I saw Diana on a corner, in shorts an Pro Keds, all smiles, cause she was high, her eyes lookin like eight balls.

"Lissen," she said. "I was wonderin if like maybe you could do me a favor and shit? Can you like turn me on to some Horse? I really wanna try it, an Sara said you'd turn me on. Whacha say, yeah?"

Somethin inside me popped. I'm not normally a violent person, but like a reflex an shit, I smacked her right in the face, hard. She fell back about three feet against a riot gate that rattled.

"Whachu do that for?" she yelled, blood burstin over her teeth from a busted lip. She was breathin heavy, like some tough butch. I juss stared at her, then went upstairs to my H. I felt bad for her motha. I felt like maybe her motha shoulda beat her up more. I wished my motha woulda cared that much for me. A good motha in life is a break, an nobody with a good break like that got a right to go lookin for H.

The Boy Without a Flag

"Man, you out already?" Smiley said one night in surprise, going through my kit. "I thoughtchu had a week's worth."

Smiley din't know thea was a tiny baby inside of me, but I knew it. I also knew thea was a part of me in that baby, an a part of him, an zero plus zero equals zero. So I din't say nothin.

I got a abortion.

BIRTHDAY BOY

It's my birthday.

I'm sittin here on my stoop, nursin my wounds. Salsa music blares. The sun's just comin up now, peekin over the rim of that abandoned buildin across the street. I gotta wait til nine fucken o'clock. The black-hole windows of the empty buildin stare at me like they wanna swallow me.

I move somewhere else. This is cause soon my father be comin down this stoop on his way to work. Mr. Movin Man, my father is. He got muscles like that Conan guy, Schwarzenegger. It's still early, but you never know, with my luck he'll come down for a muffin or some shit, an if he see me, I don't know what'll happen. My father's the real thing, an when he comes bustin in, you see your life playin in your head like a Super-8 loop. He don't make no idle threats. He talks with his fists. That's why when he said, "I'm gonna kill you!" in his boiler-room Spanish, I made for the exit, sorry I ever showed up. Send ya a postcard sometime, crabby. I feel like one a those Bowery Boys an shit.

I guess I gotta explain about my father. He's a big, bulky man. He speaks English with a hateful accent, the kind that says, "I don spee no Englitch lie ju. *Soy hispano, puñeta.*" He works as a mover for La Flor De Mayo. He's worked there twelve years. He's a supervisor now, but he's no office guy. He's still out there, sweatin up his shirts.

He was a marine in the First Division. They fought in Korea, in some big battles. He missed those battles. Two years too late. He was upset about it. He had thought bein a marine would help him career-wise when he got out, but it din't do that. It only developed his taste for liquor an oriental pussy, an he still couldn't speak di Englitch so good. He worked in restaurants, bars, even Macy's. He drank himself rabbit-eyed. He met my mother in a bar in Spanish Harlem.

My mother was a real flower, man. The pictures I saw of her make Iris Chacón look like some kinda fly shit. She had black hair down to her ass, wearin tight dresses that showed off all the curves. (I'm not makin it up, I swear, I seen the pictures.) You might've thought she was maybe some kinda hooker. You might've. But don't ever come up to me an say it, or I'll take out my six-inch an slice an dice you. I don't know why she was in a bar. Like I said, let's not talk about it. All I know is she was a real beauty, lipstick glowin like neon, a long cigarette blazin away in one hand like that German chick Marlene Dietrich. She was irresistible, a kind of movie star, leanin against the bar. Her legs weren't bad, neither. I saw them in this picture where she's on a Ferris wheel with my father, an her skirt flew up or somethin. Coulda put Raquel outta business real quick.

My father back then was kinda debonair. He was muscular. His face was long and pudgy, with a kinda boyish craziness in it. He had a thin mustache over his top lip. Sorta like Clark Gable after a few workouts at Jack LaLane's.

So they fell in love, an I popped out. We lived on Home Street. Our windows all looked out on the el. I would watch

the train clatter by an I would say, "I wanna be a train driver."
I would sit on the fire escape with breezes makin my hair fly
around, an I would look at the trains an wave, an the motormen would wave back, an I would look in an see my mother
cookin at the stove, the walls lookin moist. Her long hair
would be in a bun at the top of her head like some dancer.
There'd be chicken wings cracklin in the steamin pan. She
would lean out to me through the window an hand me a fresh
chicken wing, oil still fizzin, wrapped in a paper towel. I used
to tell her I was gonna marry her when I grew up.

My father used to take me to ball games. We used to
almost live in Yankee Stadium, with the smell of franks an
mustard, my mother wearin pointy sunglasses. He'd take me
out to Randall's Island to catch some baseballs. He used to
walk with me an my mother across the Triboro, me ridin on
his shoulders, watchin cars hum by like bullets on one side
while the river sparkled over the safety gratin on the other.
I was lucky. I was an only child, an my father was like a pal,
a buddy. He'd buy me toys an comics an gave me a weekly
allowance so I could buy baseball cards.

"So, whachu wanna be when you grow up?" he asked me
one day.

"A fireman," I said, though it was hard to choose between
trains an fire trucks.

He took me down to a fire station on Kelly Street where
gleamin red engines lay sleepin, an tall white men in huge
boots lifted me around. I tried on fire helmets, turned cranks,
an spun dials. I was really fucken spoiled.

I was eleven when it all changed.

It had somethin to do with my uncle. He was this toothy
guy named Ricardo, with a huge pompadour an roach killers.
He used to come to our place a lot. We were livin in this three-
room apartment on Union Avenue. He'd sit around in the
evenings, watchin Yankee games on TV with my father, chattin
with my mother, dukin it out with me. He was a fun guy. I

always liked him, til the day I came home early cause there was some district election or somethin. I opened the door an was comin down the hallway when I see my half-naked mother runnin out of the bedroom, clampin her robe shut. She was wearin this look on her face. When she saw me, she changed a few colors, then looked relieved. She gave me a hug. I could feel her heart beatin fast. She was breathless and all pink.

"Why you home, Angel?" she asked in her sing-song Spanish, but her voice was still kinda trembly.

"Half-day," I replied in English. "Doncha remember I tole you?" I tried lookin past her. "Pop's home?" I asked, cause I could tell somebody was in the bedroom.

"No," she said, givin the bedroom a hurried glance. "No. Ricardo's here. He's lying down. He wasn't feeling good, Angel."

Now me, I wasn't no dumb putz. I already knew about fucken an all that. A year before, I saw actual fucken. No kiddin. The real thing, I knew this crater-faced kid in my class called Louis. For fifty cents, he'd take you to the house of some guy who was screwin his mother. She was a looker, a dark Dominican with lotsa eye shadow an long hair that was always swishin. I din't need no movies after what I saw live. I felt my cock fly up like a flag, stiff an radiant, stars an stripes gleamin. No way my mother did shit like that, no fucken way!

But when I saw her face an checked out Ricardo's strange grin when he stepped outta the room, shirtless an shoeless, bucklin his belt, I knew somethin was up. I suddenly pictured the two of them in there. I saw his ass pumpin into her. I saw her bloodred nails diggin into his back.

I snuck into the bedroom while they were in the kitchen, whisperin. I walked over an felt the mattress. Damp. Kinda warm. I was siftin through the sheet like an old lady goin through her rosary when my mother walked in. She let out a shriek like a cat who had just been stepped on.

"What are you doing, what's wrong?" she blurted out, pullin me off the bed. I couldn't say nothin, I was so stunned. My face turned red an so did hers. I thought she could see the picture in my head of the Dominican lady, hair swishin behind her.

"I told you, your uncle was sick," she said, lookin bugged. "He lay down for a while."

"The sheets are wet," I said, all numb.

"He was sweatin. Go out and play for a while, okay? We have to discuss some important things."

Man, you know? If I ever get a kid, I'm never lyin to it, no matter if the kid walks in an sees me smokin a jay or knifin a dude or screwin some *putita* cause his ma's on the rag. Kids always know when you lie. They feel it. An they don't forget.

My life in the streets started around this time. I started gettin in with other kids, playin stickball until the red sun disappeared under the hummin Bruckner Express overpass. I din't wanna marry my mother no more. I met a thirteen-year-old girl called Wanda Sanchez, who hiked up her dress for me in an alley behind the school for a quarter. All my early girlfriends were older than me, cause I was rough an crazy an looked older. The first girl gave me a blow job was named Maria. She used to make it with junior high guys but made an exception for me cause I was cute. (Her words, man. I don't say shit like that.)

My mother changed. She always looked scared of me. She yelled at me more an stared at me with nervous eyes whenever I was with my father.

My father changed. He was serious, laughed less, drank more, was tired alla time. When I'd be lyin in my sofa bed in the dark livin room, I'd hear um fightin an yellin. They both got cold. The streets started smellin more like home.

One night, the shit came down. There was the usual arguin, gettin louder an louder, til the door burst open an my father came flyin out. He tripped over chair, table, stereo, an television. He turned on the light an picked me up by my shoulders, right outta bed. He was breathin hard.

"No!" my mother was screamin. "Leave him alone!" She was runnin over, her face lookin fractured.

"Was he here?" he bellowed into my face. "Was he here? Ahh?" He shook me harder and harder. He smacked my face when I din't say nothin. I landed on the bed an din't move. Blood shot outta my nose.

He grabbed my mother. He pulled her by her hair, landin a punch on the side of her face that coulda nailed Samson. She let out a crushed whimper, like a stepped-on squeeze toy. She fell into a chair by the hall an sobbed while he stood over her.

"Slut!! *Hija de la gran putaaaaa*!!"

◆ ◆ ◆ ◆

I'm sittin on another stoop down a block from my buildin, fightin the images, when I see Spider. He got his hair all newly shaved. The sides look like a wheat field, an the top of his head is square. I stared at him like I was gonna puke.

"Whass up?" he asked, slippin his hand into mine. When he pulled it away, he had left a tiny vial in my hand.

"Ahh, maaan, get away with this shit," I said, holdin it out to him.

"C'mon stupid," he said, backin up, "I'm tryin t' help you out. Doncha need some money?" He sat beside me, stretchin out his stilt-legs. "Check it out: I got me a good set-up here. There's room f' you."

Yeah, right. I was in a crack house a while back, cause sometimes you gotta sleep in strange places when friends can't come through with a crib. The place was on Tinton in a rat-eaten abandoned buildin. I was sittin in there, watchin these hollow-eyed animals puffin an suckin in that shit. Spider had said I could crash there, but after he left to do some business, I felt some guy goin through my pants while I was dozin. Swish, instant reaction, my six-inch sliced through his cheek. Felt like butter. The guy yelped an ran off. I stared at a thin bony girl with ghost eyes who was standin by the dancin candle flame.

"Buy me a hit?" she asked in a torn voice.

"Listen man," I said, beatin a rhythm with my sneaks to the salsa that blared from somewhere. "I don't wanna deal no crack."

Spider nodded, pursin his thin chapped lips. "Whachu do f' money?"

"I'll be all right. I got somethin worked out right now, on my own. A job on Fox Street."

"Wooh, my man got his own deal, goin solo, huh? Cool. Lemme juss do one more commercial break, okay? Look man, I got me a organization make Federal Express look like a fucken wagon train. I got me a fine buncha eager twelve-year-olds drivin Camaros an shit. Runners. Messengers. Delivery dudes in cars, man, can you beat that? Tint the windows so they don't get hassled. We give um drivin lessons. I got a waitin list. Kids wanna work f' me, man. I'm better than any federal program you can name. I get those kids the bread!" His eyes lit up as he pressed my arm. "I got a buncha grade-schoolers pickin up crack vials on the street. I pay um a dime a vial. Beats cans! I call that my 'entry level' position."

"Ah, Spider man, I don't wanna hear it."

"Ah man, c'mon. I ain't gonna stop buggin you, man." He let his voice trail off. "You ain't goin nowhere with these chump deals." He looked out over the street, then rose up.

"I leave it to you, lil bro. By the way, happy birfday." He slid me a jay an patted my shoulder.

Ah man, fucken guy. He remembered! I couldn't even recall tellin him. I pressed his hands for a few seconds too long.

"Ey, get off, *pato*," he said, pullin away playfully, disappearin down the street.

Spider is my support. He became my school, my education. Once things fell apart at home, there was nobody else. See, my mother left. She got sick of my father beatin on her, so she booked one day, without a word to nobody. I guess I'm old enough to accept it now, but if I ever see her I think I'd give her a swish from my six-inch just to remine her I got feelins too.

When she booked, my father flipped. He took to drinkin an beatin me from one end of the house to the other. It became a nightly thing. He brought women to the house, big heavy-thighed ladies with drunken eyes an pig squeals. I could hear um fucken. He kept sayin he was gonna kill his brother if he ever found him, an me, I was next in line after that. I couldn't stay in that place no more.

So I hung with Spider. I knew him from stickball days. He had been this older dark kid back then called Alberto Colon, but then he became a *pichón*, a thin stick of a guy with a droopin mustache an a black swagger. I seen him climbin up a buildin once, with no ladder or rope. The name Spider sorta stuck.

He found me places to stay at night, like at his cousin Romero's or a girl's place or almost anywhere he could think of when I needed it. I stayed at his house sometimes when he thought it wouldn't be too dangerous. Sometimes bullets tore in through the windows.

He took care of me. He introduced me to smoke, petty theft, assault, burglary, an girls I could fuck. He even introduced me to my steady. Her name is Gloria. She lay a real bomb on me last night. I'm still steamin about it. Check this: I'm standin in the musty stairwell with her. Our whispers bounce an echo. She tells me she got a birthday present for me. When she tells me what it is, I can't believe it.

Gloria's been my girl for almost a year. She's sixteen and

gorgeous. She got legs that Marilyn Monroe be jealous of. She got curves, slippery when wet. She got a sexual appetite that would put any guy in the hospital.

I met her cause of Spider. They lived in the same buildin. He introduced me to her one day, an I took her out for pizza cause she had on a snug pair of yellow shorts an a striped halter. Her hair looked all gold an tumbled down her back in curly squiggles. She kept sayin I was too cute for words an kept caressin my face an pullin on my hair. She couldn't believe how old I was. It turned her on. This knowin grin appeared on her face, brown eyes gleamin. We shooed flies from our slices an talked a lotta bullshit. The next day, we were squattin by this abandoned car seat on the empty lot on Prospect Avenue.

"I'm sicka bein a virgin," she said. She stabbed the earth with a twig an grinned like a thief.

"So whachu wanna do about it?"

"I don't know if you equipped t' help me," she laughed.

She waited til one night when her parents went out to party. She invited me over. We fucked like animals. She was no virgin.

I had screwed girls before, but it never meant much. It was somethin to do, an after it was over I was always struck by how ugly or stupid the bitch was. Post-coital oppression, I think they call it. Gloria was different. She put some kinda voodoo shit on my head. I couldn't stop thinkin about her. She made it too excitin. She found tons of friends whose houses were available. She'd take me to one an wear all that Hollywood stuff, stockins an garter belts an lace bras an high heels. I never saw that shit on a girl before. I couldn't get enough of her.

So about a year later, I'm standin in the hall with her. She's givin me her smile, all lust an tenderness, eyes glintin like stones.

"I got a birthday present f' you," she says, bitin her lower lip. "I don't know how you'll take it, but I'm gonna lay it on you an hope you feel the same way I do about it."

I was pressin her against me, my hands clamped around her naked waist. She had on another one of those skimpy halters, an her shorts were barely clingin to her hips.

"I'm pregnant," she said, lookin religious. "I'm carryin yuh baby, Angel!"

I stared at her.

You know, I've always thought women were all psychos, man, especially the pretty ones. I was convinced when my mother pulled her shit, an no girl I met since changed my mind. I had thought that maybe Gloria was diff, but when I saw her starin at me with that goofy holy-ghost expression on her face, I knew she was one of them.

"This a joke?" The left side of my face twitched. Oncomin violence, it said.

"No," she said, a little wary. "I'm carryin yuh baby."

She hugged me, her arms tight around my neck, til I could hardly breathe.

♦ ♦ ♦ ♦

Nine o'clock.

Last thoughts on Gloria: I can't believe that bitch! How could she bring up marriage? Is she that fucken retarded? Gives me some fucken story about how her father can hire me to work in his warehouse! Wow! A career! How could I pass it up? Bitch. They're all psychos.

There's this girl. Her name is Miriam. She's a dark-skinned Dominican girl with curly short hair. I stay over at her house sometimes when I can't dig up no place else. She lives with her parents over on Fox Street. At night, she shuts the door to her room an opens her fire escape window an there I am, up the thuddin steps. We usually fuck quietly, an I slip out, first light. Works like a charm.

She has an uncle who lives three floors up. She hates him an told me I could rob him easy. All I have to do is climb in through his fire escape window any mornin, just after nine, cause the catch is broken on it. She told me where he keeps his money, he does *bolitos* an shit. She said he has all kinda money up there from the numbers. A guy could walk off with a thousand, easy. Some sick bitch, right?

So I told her yeah, I'll do it. Why not? I need some cash. The last thing me an Spider an Shorty pulled din't fork over enough money. I figured this was worth a shot. Besides, what else could go wrong on my birthday?

So there I was, makin my way up the damn fire escape. My steps sounded too loud an clumpy. I was gettin a weird feelin, like maybe I should book, forget it. Maybe Spider could fix me up okay, like he said. I started thinkin about my father, of the last time I saw him, more than a week ago.

The night I came in, it was almost like he was waitin for me. I like to show up really late if I do come in, so maybe he's asleep, but the bastid was fucken waitin for me.

"So ya here now, ahh?" he said from the bedroom door. I was already flippin off my Keds. I was dyin to sack out on the sofa bed.

"Lemme juss ass ju somethin, *carajo*," he said, walkin over to me like a lawyer in one of those Perry Masons. "Ju tink ju can come heal anytyne ju wan, *coño*? Where ju been, ahh?"

I shook my head, lookin down on my empty sneaks.

"Ju tink ju a big man? Ahh? Bigga dan me, *carajo*?"

I felt like he was gonna hit me. I felt for my six-inch, snug in a back pocket. It was instinctive. You think I wanna cut my own pop like one of those white bastids on TV? Comes home from some rich private school an blows the family away with dad's huntin rifle. Nah, man. Can't do it. You don't cut your own father. I shook my head, hard.

"I show ju who's the big man heal!!" my father yelled,

suddenly attackin. His hard fists pounded at me like if we was in the ring.

I din't pull no knife on my pop. I ran outta there. I can't go back, not ever. As I was runnin down the stairs, I heard him scream in Spanish, "You come back, *hijo de puta*, an I'll kill you!"

Damn if this Miriam din't lay it down straight. The window was open an everythin. I slipped into the warmth, knockin over some plants. I began goin through drawers, spillin clothes an balls of socks an clumps of fresh underwear. I kept hearin a hundred different sounds that made my insides rattle. Hey! Had Spider been makin fun of me when I told him I had my own thing goin?

Boom! Just like Miriam said. Bottom drawer, right side, a thick little black case with a zipper. What's this? A whole stack of fucken bills! Eight hundred? Fucken shit!! A sudden panic filled me. It was like wantin to shit an piss at the same time. I saw myself sittin in a huge Rolls, smilin at the stooped figure of my pop walkin home from work. I was holdin up a wad of bills, openin the door for him to get in.

I grabbed the cash outta the case an headed for the window.

The two cops were walkin through the littered yard, lookin up. They seemed to spot me the minute I stepped out on the fire escape. I bolted back inside. I did a little dance in the bedroom, my nerves flippin. I din't know where to go. I finally tore though the house to the front door. I struggled with the locks, trippin over the damn police lock bar that clattered an clanged like all fucken hell. I fell on the floor, got up, opened the door a crack. Police talkies were cracklin an hissin in the hall.

I don't wanna rap about this part. I walked right into the waitin arms of those huge cops, their voices teasin like if I was a naughty lil bro. They laughed when I told um my name was Angel. I got a ride in a cop car, my first. I had cuffs on, real ones. I got to stand around in the station house on 138th Street. I met a cop named Raul, who put his arm around me an walked me to a room they call "The Tank." I got finger-printed. I got my picture taken. I joked with Raul about like what was my best side. He was tryin to stay on the serious side, but I could tell he was tryin not to laugh.

When it came to my phone call, Raul got sick of me standin there, starin at the phone.

"Who you gonna call?" he asked, holdin me by the shoulders. "Your pop? Your mom? You want me to dial? Do you know the phone number?"

There was only one person I could call. Couldn't call my pop, what with the death-warrant out on me. I wasn't about to call Gloria either, like some lil putz. I left a message for the only person I had left an sat waitin, starin at the blue walls while cops shot me curious looks. I really din't expect him to come, cause I knew he always steered clear of police stations, as if every cop in New York knew him on sight.

When he walked in, though, I din't expect the look of worry on his dark face, mixed with scorn. I stood up an din't know whether to hug him or stand there or anythin. My face got all red like I wanted to cry.

"So you'd rather do your own thing," Spider said, hands on hips.

I looked down at my sneaks.

"Big deal," he said, smilin, givin me a tap on the head. "You just thirteen, man. You'll learn. But maybe now this spirience makes you wanna work wif me. You wanna shake on it, an I take care a' you?"

I nodded, wipin at my eyes. He put his arm around me just as Raul came over, carryin a clipboard with my brand new police record on it.

SHORT STOP

—To Oona. Don't worry.
Your stop is coming.

Marty chewed on his unlit cigar and let out a string of curses.
He didn't care who heard. The succession of yellow lights he
had been crawling past all night had him ready to explode. He
eased pressure on the brake, leaned back, and let out a sigh as
the train ground down to a stop.

This had to be the worst week Marty ever had as a motorman. Five years he had been doing this shit, but this week was
definitely the worst. He started thinking about it now as the
red light bathed his cab and the train engines grew silent. The
choppy voices outside the cab caught his attention.

"So you on probation now, man?" a voice asked, words all
slurred and drunken.

"Yeah, bro. I gotta court date, man. Thass cause I'm
stupid, *carajo*. I saw it comin, but wha could I do? When it go
down, it go down. I was juss inna wrong place at the wrong
time an shit."

"Ronny sai' you pull a gun on a guy." This was a third
voice, mangled and slightly sleepy.

"Wha happen was we was on the four, ride? An Patchi an Jake was sayin lookit tha guy, lookit tha guy, less do im an shit. I knew im, so I go up to im an I say, 'Yo man, you got money? Gimme the money caw m' friend hea gotta knife.' I din't have the gun man, I din't shoot im. Tha was Jake. He juss a crazy nigga. I juss sai', CHOOM! We faw on the guy, man. Can you believe," the guy paused for a kind of dramatic effect, "the chump only had eighteen dollas on im. It was embarrassin. A'course Jake shot im. We wasn't gonna get busted f' juss eighteen dollas."

The light turned yellow. Marty gave the brake a sharp tug that made the train lurch forward. Three more stops, he was thinking, three short stops, and he'd be through, finished. His relief, Clint, would appear like a knight in shining armor. He'd wave his brake like a scepter and say, "It's yours, don't wear it out." He'd be in his car and on the way home in no time, if he could survive the walk from his car, which he'd park on 112th Street (the crack thing was just starting to catch on real good on his block, and after midnight was "rush hour"). "We gotta move," he would say every night as Melissa greeted him at the door. He chanted those words now as a flurry of green lights appeared in the misty darkness ahead. He was three short stops away from some kissin an huggin and some warm veal cutlets an fries. Three short stops.

What was it about this week that had brought out all the crazies? In five years, he'd had his share of distress calls, blowing long mournful notes on his horn to signal transit cops. There had been muggings, assaults, chain snatchings, a couple of pregnant women, some heart attacks. He had thought that he was thick-skinned and hardened, that he had seen it all, but this week made him really wanna shove this fucken job real bad. Those last few stops seemed to be getting farther and farther every time. Once he left 14th Street, everthing would start melting, slowing down.

"The Lex Local is a real pussy," Clint would tell him, his

relief and sometimes drinkin buddy when the shift got to be too much. He was a large man, an ex-boxer, something Clint felt should be a requirement for this job. Like Marty, he had done time on the Woodlawn train ("The Snake") and the #2 ("The Beast"). Compared to those lines, the Lex Local was a dream, a smooth ride with a lot of stops but a lot less trouble. When it peeled out of its tunnel and headed up to Pelham, the view from the el was beautiful, a panorama of buildings and people, lights blazing, streets calm, clusters of houses with colorful patio umbrellas, busy highways, lovely green lawns, unlike the #2, which seemed to emerge from the middle of Harlem right out onto a brick-covered desert, miles of abandoned buildings lining the horizon like hollow-eyed addicts. Marty first met Clint two years earlier, when they were both doing the Seventh Avenue line (Clint was express, Marty on the local). Back then, he would ramble on about the #6.

"I tell yuh, afta I made that sweet #6, I realized why I was a motorman," he used to say. "The #6 is a sweet piece a' pussy; all the others are juss worn out hookas." They saw each other occasionally, but when they both drew shifts on the #6 three months ago, they were ecstatic. Every time Marty would pull into Brooklyn Bridge Station just before midnight, Clint would be standing on the other end of the platform. "This is where yuh park it, sucka!" he'd yell. Sometimes they'd toss in a quick bull session, sitting together in a corner seat, munching on the mangy ends of their unlit cigars. "Was I right?" Clint asked him right away. "Is this baby a sweet piece a' pussy, o' what?"

Marty didn't have much to say about it this week. The events were snatching the words right out of his mouth. He pressed down on the brake, train hissing a complaint as it slowly made its way past a cluster of maintenance dudes out there in the darkness with their luminous flak jackets. The train entered the station quietly; the station was empty except for the baggage of a few homeless men sleeping on the benches. Marty screeched to a halt, waited for the hiss from the door release, the clatter as they slid open.

"Spring Street," the conductor's voice announced in a burst of static.

Marty cursed. That was the first thing this week that had gone wrong. Usually a motorman was paired up with a conductor and, if he was lucky, they'd get to know each other and build a cool working relationship. That hadn't happened with this particular conductor, a skinny young girl with braids and clacking beads. She looked like some college student, but she was either blind or a total idiot, because it wasn't fucken Spring Street, it was Bleecker. The station signs clearly said BLEECKER. Couldn't she read? Marty patiently waited for her voice again, biting down on his smile.

"Nex stop, Canal. Wash the closin dowas."

Canal?? No, you dumb bitch! The next stop was Spring, goddamn…No way, he wasn't touching it. He sucked on his cigar for flavor. He wasn't gonna aggravate himself. He had already done that on Monday, when he worked a rush-hour shift and had first noticed she was ahead by two stops.

"This is Fifty-ninth Street," she had announced at Seventy-seventh. Marty, who had been storing up his anger and disbelief since they left 177th Street in the Bronx, got on the intercom.

"Conducta," he said, "wake up. This is Seventy-seventh."

She got the next one wrong too. "This is Fifty-firs Street."

"Conducta," he half-screamed, "this is the motorman. Take a look outcha window, Jesus…you see what stop it is? Use yuh eyes, man. This is Sixty-eighth."

"Nex stop, Grand Central," she said, much to the hilarity of the rush-hour passengers in Marty's car.

Marty let it ride. He waited until the end of their run. He walked right up to her as she stood by the empty train, before they went back uptown. "Lissen," he said, removing his cigar, "I don't know whacher problem is, butchu betta get it straight, man. I don't know many motormens be puttin up with tha shit. But where's yuh head at? Are you fucken around o' what? You can read, right? I mean, how can you say 'Fifty-ninth' when the sign fucken say 'Seventy-Seventh Street' right in yuh face?" He maybe shouldn't have been so gruff, but he had had a bad ride. Some white guy got sick at Eighty-Sixth Street and threw up right beside his cab, causing a near-stampede that almost pulled the train out of service. He couldn't clean it until Grand Central, where he marched into the dispatcher's office for paper towels. All that way, he had to smell it. The smell was still in his nostrils as he confronted her. She nailed him with defiant hazel eyes. Her uniform was crisply ironed. She even had the hat on. (So did Marty the first week he worked.)

"Listen, busta, I know you," she said calmly. "I know where you at. I know you resent me. I met enough of you wound-up He-Man types. Say whachu want, I ain't axin f' a break. I'm hea t' stay." She shook the braids back from her face with an arrogant twitch. "Like it o' not."

Marty didn't know how to argue with logic like that. He still had that vomit swimming in his head. "It's yuh ass," he said, stepping back, holding up his brake like a peace offering. Why was he gonna bust his ass? She'll be with any number of motormen next week who wouldn't put up with that shit for a second.

He eased the train out of Bleecker Street Station, again besieged by yellow lights and, down there in the distant blackness, a red one. Why couldn't he just have his three short stops?

This same week a kid pulled a gun on him. He had heard enough horror stories to kinda expect it, but in five years of doing this shit he had never come across it. Every motorman has that feeling that someday he's gonna ride into the wrong station. Marty thought he had done exactly that the day before yesterday when he pulled into 116th Street. There three lanky teenagers sharing a crack pipe surrounded his window.

"Whassup?" the tallest one cried, zooming in towards Marty's window. "You workin haaaard?" The voice was jittery, speeded up, the eyes glassy. The kid gripped at the window with thin fingers and jumped up, trying to hook a leg around the car guard.

"Ey, cut tha shit out, man!" Marty yelled. He pumped his brake, causing a series of short gasps of pressurized air, his way of telling the conductor to hurry up and close those doors. The other two boys were laughing. They were both Hispanic, wearing large black coats and baseball caps, typical posse outfits. Their faces looked swollen and rough, as if someone had tried sanding them down.

"You talkin a me?" the tall black kid said, stepping back, chest thrust out, arms sailing backwards. "You gettin bad, nigga?"

"Shoot um," one of the others said, face cringing with a brutal ferocity. "Shoot um!"

"Wash the closin dowas," the conductor's voice said. The black kid reached into his Troop Jacket, pulling out an honest-to-God snub-nose. Too late the kids thought of jamming the doors. They jumped up and struggled with them while the black kid leveled the gun.

"No way, man," Marty said, refusing to believe it. He was waiting for the all-clear signal to light up his cab. That gun can't be real, he thought. I can't show that kid I'm scared. Marty saw his life flash by quickly. He saw the *New York Post* headline: MOTORMAN SNUFFED BY CRACK TEEN!

"No way, man," he said, shaking his head.

"Shoot um!"

"Judgemen day, bro, kiss it goo'bye!!"

"Waste th' bastid!"

"*Pa' la miel'da, brode'l!*"

"Get off the fucken doors!" Marty suddenly yelled, the clattering-shoving-screaming starting to get to him, the gun muzzle looking down on him like an eye. Marty suddenly got his all-clear. He jerked the train forward. The gun went click. The tunnel wiped the image of the kids away like the shutter on a camera, but his hands were trembling, heart pounding in his head.

He put the memory away as he rumbled into Spring Street Station, empty except for a homeless refugee camp at his end of the station. There, three men had pitched a home-made tent and were lying on blankets, diggin food out of some fast-food containers. One of the men, stooped and limping, came over to Marty's window, his face as sooty as if the man had just emerged from a mine shaft. He took out a bent stublet of cigarette and put it to his lips as he leaned closer. "Yuh gotta light?" he asked, his voice strong and clear, pushing past the filthy clothes. Marty reached under his pocket and took out a cheap lighter. He lit the cigarette carefully as the man leaned into the window.

"Thanks, man," the guy said, puffing appreciatively. "Why doncha light up yuh stogie?" He motioned at the brown stub of cigar clenched between Marty's teeth. Marty laughed as he pumped the brake. "Man, doncha know yuh not allowed to smoke down hea?"

He grinned to himself as he entered the dark sloping walls of the tunnel, the rumble and squawk of the train wheels somehow reassuring. He was almost there. Two more short stops. He breathed a sigh of relief, thought of that warm veal cutlet, nicely breaded, wrapped in foil, his sweet honey lighting candles. Yeah, this'll be the year we have a kid, man; it's gotta be. Three years of tryin. Marty didn't mind the tryin, not one bit, but his folks was startin to get weird.

Canal next. Just two stops away, and the lights were all green, smooth sailing. Marty leaned into the brake as if he could pull the train himself over the rails. A short stop, man, and he'd be there. Clint would be on the other side, pointing at the yellow line on the edge of the uptown platform. "Park it hea, sucka." A few words, then home. SPLASH—into Canal at forty, lights blinking past, sliding up to the ten-car marker, where he jerked to a stop with a screech. The light was green, waiting for him. He stared at it, stroking his stubble, when he noticed the woman, sitting just beyond the light, in the tunnel's darkness. Her legs dangled down off the maintenance catwalk.

"Hey," he yelled, sticking his head out the window, "Come on, now! Get outta thea! You wanna get killed?"

The woman didn't move. Her sneakers looked like they belonged to a little girl sitting in a big chair. She had large round eyes and a bush of kinky hair that swirled down one side of her long face, dark and waxy.

"Come on, man," Marty said angrily. "Aw, shit…" His veal cutlets were getting cold, the fries moist and soggy. "Are you crazy?"

"Canal Street nex," the conductor said. "Wash the closin dowa."

Tonight she was behind a stop.

"Conductor, hole up, hole up," Marty said into his intercom mike. The doors burst open with a cranky grinding. Marty came out and stepped over to the large, dirty light, still green. The woman jumped down. She seemed to be swallowed up by the dingy darkness. She tripped on something, then stood up, balancing herself on a large tie, hands wrestling together in front of her.

"No. Doncha hurt me," she said in a husky staccato burst. Marty sighed, peeling off his engineer glove and twisting it in his hands. "Come on, lady," he urged, gesturing her back up, "you don't know whachu doin."

"I wanna die," she said. "I wan you run me ova."

"I ain't gonna move. Now come up from thea."

The woman's face collapsed. Her thin bony face, gleaming with sweat, convulsed, folding up like a paper bag. She stood her ground, gripping her elbows, eyes moist with tears. "I can't take it. Please juss run me ova."

Fucken shit. Where was the damn conductor? Couldn't the bitch see somethin was up? Marty felt angry for having to deal with this.

"Run me ova!" the woman suddenly yelled at him, her eyes resentful.

There were no passengers in his car. Who could tell if there were any on the goddamn train at all? He was standing there, cursing, feeling like somebody left him holding the bag. Then he stepped down off the catwalk, jumping down right in front of the chugging, simmering train, headlights making him feel like he was on stage. The woman cringed and scurried backwards. She tripped and fell, but Marty got there in time to cushion her fall and keep her clear of the electrified third rail. She was trembling, convulsing from a sudden fit of sobbing. "I can't take this no longa," she moaned, burying her face in his sweatshirt. Marty shushed her and tried forcing her up, but she resisted, so he squatted there precariously, one foot on the silver rail. "Come on," he said gently, "yuh gotta get up, gotta try."

"I'm sick of fightin," she mumbled. Her large eyes looked into his a moment, then some kind of embarrassment forced her to look down. This close, Marty noticed this wasn't no woman, juss some girl, some tender-face brat who should be studyin at home for a math quiz or somethin.

"How come you wanna die?" he mumbled, half to himself. "You juss a baby." No answer. He lifted her up and helped her up onto the catwalk. She was covering her face, looking away from him. He clambered up and escorted her into the empty car, which was making hollow hissing sounds. He settled her into the corner seat facing his cab. Her hands trembling, she hid her face from the lights, snot covering her upper lip. "I din't want this," she said.

"You sit there," Marty said. "I'll fine you help." He passed her a packet of tissues from inside the cab, pressed in his brake, gave off a few spurts of pressurized air. The train came back to life, sputtering and chugging. The doors slid shut. He stared at her a moment as she lay crumpled in the corner like a sack of garbage. Marty asked her where she lived as tunnel lights flashed past, but there was no answer. He shoulda guessed it from the tattered clothes, the ratty sneakers, the caked dirt around her ankles. The murky tunnel walls raced past as he got on the radio. "This is Pelham ten-fifty. I gotta woman hea needs medical assistance." The radio crackled harshly. "Damn it, yeah. A cop then. I'm comin in to Bridge now." The radio hissed again. "No, nah, I din't say that. I said I gotta woman hea need a docta." An angry cough from the speaker. "No." Marty's voice got smaller. "Lady vagrant. Girl vagrant. Out on the tracks." His shoulders sagged a little as he replaced the receiver. He shot her a look as she wiped at her face with the tissues. He wanted to say he was going to help her, but he couldn't say anything.

When he entered Brooklyn Bridge Station, he was hardly aware of it. His hands worked automatically. He braked a little too early and had to crawl up to the ten-car marker in small screeching lunges.

"This is Canal—no, correction, this is Brooklyn Bridge, lass stop. All passenjahs off."

Funny how she always got the last stop right, wasn't it? Maybe it was all she could see, the last stop, the one she lived for. Maybe she was just like him after all. He disengaged his brake with a grunt, stepping out of the cab and over to the girl. She looked at him with empty eyes. "I wanna die," she said.

"Come on," Marty said, helping her up on her feet, walking her off the train. Her steps were uncertain and slow. She didn't seem drunk or high, just ashamed of something. She kept her hand over her eyes, as if shielding them from the light. A pair of large transit cops appeared, hairy arms hooked on their belts. They had weary features and sleep-starved faces.

"So whass this?" the first one asked. "Goin f' walks inna

The Boy Without a Flag

tunnel?" He stepped close, peering into her face. "You on anythin, honey?" They both seemed reluctant to touch her when
Marty let go of her, and she tipped and swayed. Marty tried
bringing her hands away from her face, but they kept going
back up, slowly. "Look, these guys'll take care a' yuh," he said,
but his voice was gone. He reluctantly told the cops the story,
then got back in the cab and buzzed the conductor, who shut
the doors. He pumped the brake and jerked out of the station,
rolling down the circular stretch of track that brought him
back into the station on the uptown side. He sailed in, braking
with a wail and a rude bumping. He disengaged the brake.
The train let out a loud gasp, its four 100-horse-power traction
motors beating out a thumping tattoo that abruptly died.
When the doors opened, Clint was right there. His face had a
cautious grin on. "My man," he said, holding out his hand,
"you still park a mean sum'bitch." Marty almost walked past
him for a moment, his eyes scanning the downtown side.
He was looking for the two cops and the girl, but he couldn't
see them.

"Whassup, bro?" Clint asked, knowing something was
wrong because Marty had that strange look on his face, part
anger, part fear, like the time he had gone through that gun
thing. Marty didn't answer. He was now staring at the girl, who
he spotted carefully working her way down the platform. She
was a tiny apparition that swiftly vanished into the tunnel, right
at the point where trains come speeding down a sharp curve,
entering the station at almost uncontrollable speeds. No motorman in the world would be able to stop the 800,000 pound
snake. She'd only be a quick flash, a snapshot of a face to the
unlucky motorman, who would brake and still be carried forty
yards by sheer momentum, long past the point where there
would be anything remotely recognizable as human staining
the undercarriage of the gasping, hissing beast.

"Damn," Marty said. He took the cigar out of his mouth
and tucked it in a pocket. Clint stood there, not pushing it.

"Still havin a bad week?" he asked finally as he turned and walked into the train.

"The worst," Marty said, heading for the stairs to the other side. Clint watched him rush past as if he had an errand. He had wanted to say, "Hey! Don't wear it out," but he could already see that it was wore to the bone.

THE LOTTO

Another sleepless night.

Dalia kept having the same bad dream. She wished she could tell her mother about it, but she couldn't. She sat by the window and bit her lip.

Her mother was always asking her if she'd had any Lotto dreams, especially this week, with the fifty million dollar pot in the balance. Dalia would run through her dream bit by bit while her mother whipped some eggs into froth. "You said there were how many men with beards?" she'd ask, deriving a number from inane symbols. Her mother believed in the power of dreams. She believed God was going to disclose to her the winning numbers.

Dalia wasn't so sure about dreams, but now that this horrible dream kept coming back, she couldn't help feeling that God was trying to tell her something. Three times in seven days she'd had the dream. In the dream, she was sitting in a waiting room that looked like a small theater. On a stage facing her were several doctors in white smocks and surgical masks. In front of them was a table on which sat three top hats. The doctors kept reaching into the hats, pulling out babies with resounding pops. The babies were handed to nurses who waited nearby and wore elbow-high surgical gloves. Dalia always began to cry with horror and to scream for Ricky, but he was nowhere to be found. This last time she was whimpering like a puppy when she woke up. She sat by the window, listless breezes caressing her. Definitely one dream she couldn't tell her mother about.

The street below was alive with activity even though it was three-thirty in the morning. Dealers leaned into double-parked cars. A young girl with a scarred face swung her ass at passing cars, her silver shorts sparkling as headlights swept past. Next to her was a guy in ratty jeans that Dalia recognized. He was a quiet kid with a cratered face named Careta, which is Spanish for "funny-face." He was the first person she had seen since Ricky vanished five days ago who might know where he was.

Dalia quickly slipped on some clothes. She scooped her keys off the dresser and slipped out on sneakered tippytoes, creeping quietly past her parents' room, her father's snoring coming through the shut door. She didn't want to think of what would happen if they discovered her sneaking out like that. She thought instead of the glistening baby bodies coming out of top hats. That made her walk faster. She came right up to Careta and put it to him, but Careta was evasive. He hardly looked her in the eyes and made cigarette smoke clouds that swirled around her like fog. (Dalia hated cigarettes.) He was a kid of few words, but he managed to get irritated enough to spit out a torrent of them before he jetted. "Lookit," he said, finally nailing her with his cave-dweller eyes, "I don't know where he is. I know he's hidin, thass all. You shunt ax why. He's juss involved in some shit, thass all. He bit off more than he could chew." The words seemed to be aimed right at her, like torpedoes.

She thought of the last time she had seen Ricky, five days ago. It was just after the first time she had the dream. They were both standing in the building stairwell after a disastrous date where she wouldn't let him touch nothin. She told him about the dream. When he didn't get the message, she told him more, about throwing up and being weak-kneed and dizzy and scared. His answer was to light a cigarette. He never did that in front of her because he knew she hated it. She wouldn't kiss him, and he'd have to suck on breath mints. Now he was puffing away and the smoke screen engulfed her.

"When you gonna know bout this shit f' sure?" he asked petulantly.

"I don't know."

"You don't know? Wha kinda shit is that? A girl's suppose t' take care a' this shit, man. You blew it big time, you stupid…"

"It's not all my fault," she said, hating the way her voice quivered. "I din't do it alone." She stared at his contorted face, disgusting smoke pouring out of his mouth. She hated him, hated that she had made love to him. She shoulda neva opened her legs for him! She fought off the tears. She didn't want him to think she was crying for him, she was just angry with herself for letting such a bastid fuck her. The tears started coming out just as a whole family came trooping down the stairs. Plump chattering adults clacked past, children in thumping sneakers bringing up the rear. They all turned to look as they passed.

"Come on, man! Don't cry, you embarrassin me," Ricky whispered angrily. He leaned on the far wall as if he didn't know her. He waited for all the noise to die down, for the vestibule door to screech shut. Then he said, "I gotta go." He dutifully kissed her, then briskly hopped down the stairs with quick clumpings. And that was the last time she had seen him.

As she sneaked back upstairs into her dark room, she thought of how much time she had spent trying to decide if she was going to fuck him or not.

"I say go for it," Elba had said to her in "their" pizzeria on Wales Avenue. Elba, a short, curvy girl with dark, curly hair tumbling down to her shoulders, was in Dalia's homeroom. This past semester they had become close friends, holding unofficial races to see who would get a boyfriend first. Dalia lost, but when she caught up they began exchanging notes and observations. Elba's first boy was a thin basketball player named Jose, while Dalia smooched with a pudgy jock named David. They soon grew bored and moved on, always comparing like shoppers. Elba always got more boyfriends, but that was because she was a loudmouth and wore tight blue slacks that showed off her sweet ass like the taut skin on a plum. She talked real loud, catty and chatty, and if you din't like it, fuck you, she'd say, eyes flashing a challenge. Dalia was meek. Maybe she braided her shiny hair and wore skirts with the panty hose that had designs on the thighs, but she wasn't catty or chatty. Her prettiness was more of a private affair, something you'd spot in the way she smiled or the way she put her face close to the paper whenever she wrote anything, her hair cascading gently. She was pickier than Elba. This was because she read a lot of romance books. The young toughs who tamed their streetwalk around her and bought her slices of pizza before locking her in a half nelson in the balcony at The Prospect didn't stand much of a chance, which was why Ricky was such a problem. She wondered if maybe she had done it with him because of Elba's decision one night to up the ante in their contest by having sex. She had, by this time, been seeing the same guy for close to a year, on and off.

"But do you love the guy?" Dalia had asked as they sat at a greasy table in the pizzeria, a nearby video game whirring and beeping.

"I don't know," Elba said, munching thoughtfully on her slice. "It's nah tha easy to tell an shit."

"But you should know, shouldn't you?"

Elba shrugged. "I been wif the guy long enough, girl. I know I'm crazy about him. But he's gettin antsy."

"Antsy?"

"Yeah, you know." Her eyes flashed. "Yesterday I caught him inna hall outside Mr. Baumann's class. His hands were holdin Teresa DelRio." Dalia frowned. Teresa was the junior-high tramp. She got up to yawn one day in math class, stretching her cat-like body, rubbing her ass against the desk behind her. "I love sex," she said, "can't get enough." Every boy in class heard it. The scores for the surprise quiz on polynomials that morning were abysmal. "If I don't do it, he'll go somewhere else," Elba said with a mouthful of pizza. One of her long curls fell into the slice as if tasting it.

"But that's no reason to do it, is it?" Dalia waited for an answer, wide-eyed, but Elba only munched and grinned and shook hair off a shoulder. The video game buzzed and beeped, the young guy in front of the screen swerving, his hand banging into buttons. "He that important to you? You get boyfriends all the time. When you fight with him, you go on the prowl. Why does he matter so much now?"

Elba shrugged. She was biting into her slice and suddenly froze, a dazed look on her face. "I don't know," she said.

"What if you get pregnant?"

The video game let out a series of loud explosions. "Damn!" the young guy yelled, slamming his palm against the dashboard of his dead star-cruiser. There was a funeral march.

Elba scowled. "I won't get pregnant. You see too much 'General Hospital.' "

Elba didn't get pregnant. She had sex and liked it and had more sex and began liking it more and more. She urged Dalia to find someone to do it with. Was that why she had done it with Ricky? This question kept popping up. It was like indigestion. Dalia didn't want to admit to herself that maybe she did it so she wouldn't lose Elba, who was now walking on a higher plane. All she talked about was fucking. She hung out with other girls now too, even Teresa DelRio. It seemed like some exclusive club, this womanhood deal. Dalia felt left out, the younger sibling tagging along with the bigger girls.

So maybe that's why she had chosen Ricky. So what? She knew him from seeing him hanging out on Prospect Avenue with his goon pals. There they were, shattering the glass on a bus stand, their peals of laughter echoing down Southern Boulevard. There they came, running past her window, chasing a skinny Mexican kid from the fifth floor who had his paycheck punctually stolen every Friday. Ricky always smiled at her. He winked. He had a mustache, but it was baby fuzz. They began exchanging words. He had a childlike way of pointing with his chin, eyes twinkling luminously. Whenever he popped up in front of her on the street, she'd get a nervous look in her eyes. She'd look down as if trying to hide her smile behind her shoulder.

One day she was in the pharmacy taking in her mother's Lotto forms when he crept up behind her and gave her a huge red lollypop. He offered to take her to the movies. "Which one?" she asked, not looking at him. He leaned against the counter and didn't look at her either. "Somethin romantic. Maybe *Rambo III*." Dalia told her mother she was going to Elba's house, even though she hadn't seen Elba for two weeks. Elba was too busy with her steady boyfriend and the world of sex to be much excited by one of Dalia's schoolgirl status reports.

Ricky met her on the stoop wearing a clean big shirt and gray chinos. Even his wild bushy hair was combed neatly. A batch of his friends watched them from their spot by the bodega, faces solemn. "For you," he said, handing her a new pack of Starbursts. She remembered seeing parts of *Rambo III* in between all the kissing and pressing, the taste of lipstick and popcorn. On the way back, her legs felt weak and springy, her eyes dreamy and stoned. Despite the petting, Ricky was pretty respectful. His hands roamed but stayed in all the roaming places, and this made her like him even more. It took two weeks before she got into bed with him. By that time, she had already spoken to Elba about it. They had one of their special meetings, slices of pizza steaming on their table.

"Go for it," Elba said nonchalantly. "It's no big deal once you get used to it." She was examining her long red nails. "You scared?"

"No," Dalia lied. She laughed and Elba gripped her hands. Elba seemed like an older sister now. She wore make-up and cut her hair some and took to wearing more skirts with glittering panty hose and pumps. Her eyes looked kind of chinky from the eyeliner. "Go for it," she said. "Lemme know wha happens."

Ricky took her to some guy's house, a crack dealer who worked nights. His tiny crib was on Jackson Avenue, overlooking the el. The sun was still out when Ricky first got a look at her frilly see-thru panties, which she had bought with Elba at Alexander's on Third Avenue. Ricky was real gentle. He hadn't smoked all day, so his kisses tasted like cherry Chapstick. He cradled her like a little girl and stopped when it hurt. They stopped and started all night without even eating, and it felt better and better. Just before midnight he was still fucking her, and the clattering trains that passed filled the dark room with flickering strobe lights.

"Ma?" she said into the phone, trying to pull Ricky's mouth away from one of her nipples. "Yeah, I know. Elba's ma says I could maybe stay over tonight? It got later than I planned."

"Did you drop off the Lotto forms for me?"

"Yes."

"Don't lose the stubs. The drawing is tomorrow."

The next night, she felt sick. She didn't know if it was guilt over all that fucking, or whether it was just nerves because she had read about morning sickness and she had had that, puking up quietly in the bathroom with the door shut and the tap water running. She looked at her mother's wrinkled face and wondered if God would snitch on her.

"I had a dream last night," she could hear her mother saying with a grim face. "I had a dream you did something very bad, and maybe now you're sick." She sat on the couch beside her father, who was reading *El Diario* while the TV blared; it was the start of the World Series. Dalia's mother, in the kitchen washing dishes, occasionally stepped over into the living room, gripping a dripping pan. "Don't forget, the drawing," she'd say every ten minutes. Her father, paragon of patience, kept quiet, but finally he yelled, "Cut it out already. I can't stand you going on about this shit." He had a stern rock-hard face. Like a President's face on Mount Rushmore.

"Watch the way you talk!" she yelled from the doorway. "You want God to punish us for your lack of faith?" He looked up from his paper. She came closer, pointing a dripping pan at him. "God punishes us every time you let loose with that mouth of yours. Remember last week? Two numbers short! If only you'd believe a little!"

"I can't believe," he yelled, tossing down the paper, "that I sit behind a little window eight hours a day and sell people stamps so you can spend ten bucks a week on the fucking Lotto." He glared at Dalia, who felt like puking. "I hope you're not getting like your mother. I hear you every morning, telling her your Lotto dreams. Does God send you secrets in your dreams, too, or what?" He shook Dalia's arm. "You getting as cracked as Rosa here?"

"Camilo!" Dalia's mother screamed. She had gone back to the kitchen during his harangue but now returned. "It's time! The drawing!" She ran over to the TV, drying her hands on her apron frantically.

"I'm scared," Dalia told Elba a week later. They were sitting in a children's park across the street from their school. She told Elba about being sick and scared and about the way Ricky was losing his interest in her, and it was good in a way because he was a stupid dipshit, and she shoulda neva done it with him, but it was bad because she had and now she was like this.

Elba leaned back against the bench and stared up at the murky sky. "Oh boy," she said, her hands buried in her jacket pockets.

"You think I did a 'General Hospital'?" Dalia asked softly. They both watched a trio of boys jump up on a slide, toppling down its silvery smoothness one right after the other.

Elba sighed, pursing her lips as if she were sucking on a lemon. "You better tell this jerk real quick," she said quietly.

The morning Dalia met Ricky to tell him, she had the dream. She figured it was just nerves. She had called his house several times to leave messages. That was the only way to get him. He was never there. Somehow he always got the messages, always called back. But what if he didn't want to? When he got back to her, they set up a date, but it was more like a pretend-date. They had pizza and walked around and even did some necking, but he tasted like Winstons, and she was too nervous to get into it. They ended up in the stairwell.

After he vanished, the dream came back. She kept seeing the slick, quivering baby bodies and kept hearing Rosa's voice: "Whenever God wants to tell you something, he'll put it in a dream, and if you don't get the hint, he'll make it come back again and again. So let me know if you have any dreams like that, because it could be God trying to give us Lotto numbers."

After Careta failed her, she lay in bed staring at the ceiling until dawn came. "I've got to see Elba," she thought. She hadn't seen her since Ricky went poof. "She'll know what to do."

She slept late, got up at one with her eyes feeling like prunes. When she walked into the kitchen, she found her mother sitting at the kitchen table with her magic box. It was a wooden box with carved angels on it and rusty latch that Rosa had found in the mountains of Jayuya when she was twelve. It was a lucky box, filled with a lifetime of lucky trinkets, a rabbit's foot and a rooster claw that burned evil spirits and a pair of dice her brother Martino had won four thousand dollars with in Korea. She had a batch of Lotto tickets in there. This was because whenever she felt uncertain about something, she'd stick it in the box with the lucky things. Dalia remembered that Rosa had done it once with an electric bill Camilo had been worried about. She had put it in the box the minute Dalia brought it in. The next morning, after Camilo had left for work, she brought the box over and took the envelope out of it and told Dalia to open it. Inside Dalia found a notice informing them that because of a computer error they had overpaid their last bill and now had credit.

"You see?" Rosa had said, petting her hand. "You must have faith! Too bad your father isn't here to see this!"

Dalia sat down beside her, rubbing her eyes while Rosa fiddled with her Lotto forms. "You look tired," she said. She held up two of the forms. "Any Lotto dreams?"

Dalia bit her lower lip. "Nah. Nothing." She blushed. She felt as if her mother would be able to sense God was sending her signals of some kind, but her mother just handed her a pair of forms.

"I had one the other night," Rosa whispered. "I've never had such an intense dream! Migdalia, it's going to happen! Fifty million dollars!" Dalia smiled, chin in hand, Lotto forms blurring in front of her. "Let me tell you about this dream. I'm standing by this huge scaffold with all these people from my town, even dead ones, like Nydia Fernandez, who was hit by a cement mixer. Anyway, we're standing around, and these soldiers appear, bringing with them this bearded man. It dawns on all of us that he is being put to death! So, as the noose is going around his neck, he stoops over to where I am and says, 'Look, this is the only time I'll get to tell you, so listen well: sixteen, two, four, seventeen...' And then there was this other dream where I'm on the street playing marbles, only I'm fully grown, and—"

"Ma, I gotta make a call," Dalia cut in, not wanting to stay for the punch line.

"What I want to ask you is can you take these Lotto forms over to the pharmacy today?" Her mother's eyes gleamed. She was holding up the Lotto forms as if they were train tickets.

"Sure. No problem." Dalia gave her a kiss on the head, declining offers of food. Her stomach was still rumbling, her head dizzy. She phoned Elba's, but only got her mother, who said Elba had left the house looking grim. Dalia left a message and got dressed. She started thinking of how her parents would take the news that she was about to have the baby of a street punk. Her father would get angry and yell, her mother would cry and ask God why. She hated the feeling in her head, the weakness in her limbs. She could almost feel something growing inside of her, like a plum pit stuck in her throat. She called Ricky's. He wasn't there. "Do you know when he'll be back?" she asked in her jittery Spanish. "No *tengo* idea," the terse wheezing voice replied. The line went dead.

She left the stuffy apartment with the Lotto cards in her hand. She wandered up Southern Boulevard, looking into pizzerias and bodegas where she knew Ricky sometimes hung out. She stopped by a laundromat on Avenue St. John where she had caught him many times rapping to girls. She crossed through an empty lot and went down Prospect all the way to the el station because she knew sometimes Ricky and posse terrorized passengers coming off trains by swinging sticks at them and shoving them down stairs. Nothing. Not a single face tied to Ricky. He had disappeared and taken all his friends with him.

She came back down Prospect, up 149th Street. She was

heading for the pizzeria on Wales, where she and Elba always had their chats. She was just reaching it when she saw Elba in a black skirt and large jacket, hair tumbling down onto her shoulders in dark round coils. She seemed distraught, almost shivering as she stood outside the pizzeria, arms folded across her chest. Dalia's heart began to pump loudly in her ears. She raced across the street. The minute Elba spotted her, she let out a tiny yell. "Damn, I was thinkin boutchu right now," she said. "Thass weird."

"What are you doing here?"

"I don't know. How'd it go wif yuh boyfriend?"

Dalia's face darkened. "Ever since I told him, he's been gone. Even his friends." She shrugged. "Five days ago."

"Didju find out if yuh—"

"Don't even say it."

"Butchu don't even know?"

"I don't think I wanna."

Elba grabbed her by the arm and steered her into the warm pizzeria. "Come on. Pizza time."

Dalia sat down by the warbling, humming video game while Elba ordered some slices. She thought that Elba looked a little funny around the eyes, like maybe she hadn't been sleeping. As Elba sat down, she also noticed that the polish on her nails was chipped, something very un-Elba-like. "Look," Elba said commandingly, "we can't fuck around. This is real serious shit, okay? I love you an everythin, but you can't sit around. You gotta take a test."

Dalia sighed. "Planned Parenthood?"

Elba's face seemed to shrink for a fraction of a second. "Nah," she said, playing with her straw wrapper. "You ain't got time. You gotta get a quick test. One of those instant things, like in the pharmacy. I shoulda done that. Shit." She looked away disgustedly.

"You?" Dalia's eyes widened.

"Come on, try the fucken slice. Paid money for it, you

know." She bit down on the crust with a crunch. Elba always started with the crust. Dalia stared at her slice and felt as if she were falling into that greasy sea of sauce and cheese. She couldn't. "Tell me what's going on, Elba."

Elba grinned tiredly, her eyes evasive. She suddenly gripped Dalia's hand, then took another bite of the crust. She wasn't looking at Dalia at all. "I got an appointment," she said.

"Really?" There was fear and admiration in Dalia's voice. It made Elba look at her for a moment, but not for too long, because she was in that fragile place where any small thing might bring tears. Her eyes were sore from that stuff already. She inhaled deeply. "Yeah. Today at three. I've rescheduled twice. I keep chickenin out, but I got to go. I was standin outside, thinkin maybe I wanted t' call you, an there you are." Something in her voice broke. Her eyes got watery. She tried not looking at Dalia, but Dalia got up and sat beside her and pulled her closer and that did it. Elba began to sob convulsively. It only lasted a moment, because of the pizza guy twirling his dough, and the two guys by the window chomping on slices, and that counterboy in the red-striped shirt munching gum and staring. In no time, she was wiping her face and shaking her head and half-laughing. She caught the sparkle in Dalia's eyes for a moment, but Dalia quickly applied the pizza napkin. "You want I should come with you?"

Elba patted her hand. "Nah. Betta if I go alone, I think. But maybe I drop by yuh house later?"

"Yeah, you better."

"An you girl, we gonna getchu a test. We do it now, while I'm around. We'll go to the pharmacy an buy it. Butchu gotta take it tonight. When I go ova t' yuh house, if you din't take it, I won't tell you about my...news."

Dalia sighed. "Okay. You got a deal." They shook on it. They both walked to the pharmacy, feeling a little quiet. When they got to the corner of Southern Boulevard and 149th, they saw the Lotto line stretching from the pharmacy entrance to the supermarket doorway three stores down. Dalia got right in line while Elba went in to buy the test for Dalia. This was because Dalia was known by a lot of people in the store, and if they saw her buying that, they'd talk, and the talk might get to her mother. Elba didn't have that problem. She bought the test and came right back. "No sweat," she said, handing her the package. "This one takes thirty minutes." She was going to take it out of the bag for Dalia to show her, but Dalia yanked it away.

"Damn man," Elba said, laughing, "it's not like you got leprosy an shit."

After that little laugh, Elba got kind of grim because her appointment was coming up. Dalia gave her a hug and reminded her to come by the house. Elba rolled her fingers under Dalia's chin as if tickling her. "See ya wif the verdick." Dalia watched Elba walk off down the street, getting smaller and smaller until the traffic seemed to swallow her up. She stood in that line for close to forty minutes, behind a fat man who kept blowing his nose with pink tissues that he dropped on the sidewalk. Rosa was waiting for her when she got home. She took the ticket stubs and tucked them right into her box. She made a funny face and crossed her fingers. "Tonight's the night," she said.

Dalia went into her room. She took the package out of her jacket pocket and stuck it deep inside a drawer, as if she planned never to see it again. She knew she had made a deal with Elba and all, but she was thinking that maybe she could take the test when Elba arrived. After all, it took only thirty minutes! She changed into her bummy clothes and went into the kitchen to help her mother prepare dinner. Camilo worked until noon on Saturdays, but then came the weekly domino tournament outside Pellin's bodega on Southern Boulevard, he and three others sitting on crates, downing beers, playing for money. It was an outdoor event that sometimes moved to the back room when it was chilly.

By the time he tramped in wearing his weary face, Dalia had already taken the test. She had done it in the bathroom because she was sick of the babies coming out of hats while she was peeling potatoes and chopping onions. She hid the little vial behind a pair of old paint cans under the basin.

"I tell you," Camilo said, searching in the refrigerator for a beer, "we better win that fucking Lotto tonight because I didn't have a good night at dominoes."

Rosa frowned. "I don't believe you! How could you? Tonight being so special."

"Special? Get out of here with that. There's a drawing every damn Saturday."

"Not for fifty million dollars! And you, gambling!"

"What the hell you think a Lotto is, a religious event? The damn World Series is on."

"Camilo, put the drawing on," Rosa said urgently. "Put it on now, before the game, please! I don't want to miss it. We can't." Camilo popped his beer open and took a sip and went into the living room.

"I live in a nuthouse," he muttered, flipping on the TV.

Rosa hurried into the kitchen to retrieve her magic box, which was on the refrigerator and had the stubs inside.

"You'll miss the Lotto, honey," Rosa said urgently to Dalia, who was turning the rice.

Her stomach was churning. She knew that her test results were waiting. The verdict was already in. She stood by the doorway to the kitchen, watching as her parents sat in front of the TV, the blazing screen bouncing light off the walls. Rosa was holding all her ticket stubs in her hand.

"Give me the tickets." Camilo made a grab for them.

"No. I'll hold them. Camilo!"

"Get a paper! Write the numbers down!" he screamed. The two of them fumbled over each other as Dalia stood behind them, her senses twitching. Her hands involuntarily grasped her tummy where all the trouble was.

On the screen was a blond woman, pale features stark against the orange and blue background. In front of her was a huge machine resembling a corn popper. Inside hopped and spun dozens of white golf balls, each printed with a number. When the woman pressed a button, a ball would be sucked up a thin tube, appearing atop a kind of funnel.

"And the first number is three," she said.

"*Ay Cristo*," Rosa moaned, waving one of the many tickets she was holding. Camilo was trying to snatch it. "*Carajo*, I don't believe it," he said loudly.

"Shut up with the cursing!" Rosa screamed, punching him. "You'll blow it for all of us!"

"The next number is sixteen." The camera zoomed in on the ball.

"Goddamn," Camilo said, shaking the ticket. He was hopping up and down, inching closer to the screen. He shot Dalia an amazed look.

"Seven, the next number is seven."

Camilo turned up the volume on the set. The cheesy Lotto electronic music boomed through the room. It was like a video game theme.

"*Ay dios, ay dios…*" Rosa was chanting, her nails digging deep into Camilo's wrist.

"I'll never laugh at your dreams again," he vowed in a deep voice, "if only…oh Jesus…"

Dalia backed away from it. She ran into the bathroom. The cheesy Lotto music was still playing. She shut the door hard and turned on the tap water full blast, until she couldn't hear anything but the roar of the water and her heart hammering away in her head. She knelt down under the basin, her hand searching for the vial. Her fingers closed in on its smoothness. Her heart seemed to jump for just a second. The room filled up with steam. She held the vial up to the light. Short gasps escaped her. She stared and stared at it from all sides, her hands trembling. Then she climbed up on the toilet and forced the tiny window open, her eyes clouding with tears. Gusts of cold air struck her face like hard slaps. She checked the vial one last time, then threw it as hard as she could. She shut the window and turned off the water and watched it glisten in the tub. She pulled open the door, cool air sweeping over her as she stepped out of the humidity and into the living room. It was almost as if she were coming out of some dream.

A massive cheer greeted her. It filled the whole room. A stadium of people were standing on their feet, stomping and screaming, players rounding the bases. On the couch sat Camilo, face drawn, staring at the game vacantly. A beer sweated in one hand. The torn scraps of the Lotto tickets lay scattered all over the couch beside him. He turned to look at Dalia and noticed her face was all wet.

"Ah shit, not you too. I'm stuck with a pair of loonies. You and your stupid dreams," he said resentfully. The words made her start gasping for breath again, her chest wracked with sobs.

Rosa appeared at the door, her face also red. She came over to Dalia and hugged her. "It's okay, it's okay," she said in English. "God still cares." At the sound of those words Dalia exploded, tears of relief and gratitude overwhelming her. She was laughing and crying at the same time, so that Rosa pulled back to look at her.

"It was so close," Dalia said, but she looked relieved.

"Next time it's the real thing," her mother said soothingly. "Just have faith." Rosa shot Camilo a look, but he was facing the baseball game as if they didn't exist.

When the door buzzer sounded, Dalia jumped. "I'll get it," she told Rosa, scampering past the kitchen into the hall, where the intercom was.

"Guess who," Elba's voice came over the speaker.

"Come on up. Hurry!" Dalia said, unlocking the door, standing out in the hallway listening to Elba's sneakers thumping up the stairs. In no time, Elba was standing in front of her. She gripped Dalia's arms anxiously. "Well?"

"You tell me first!" Dalia almost screamed.

"Fuck you! I came up here," Elba said angrily, "Now spill it, girl!"

"I'm not, I'm not, I'm not!" Dalia jumped in the air and gave Elba a tight, tight hug that made her let out a kind of squeaking noise. Elba's arms wrapped slowly around her, fingers gripping. "I knew it," she said into her ear, "I knew you wasn't! Din't I tell you not t' worry? I gotta instic' about this shit! I'm happy f' you, runt!"

They embraced, Dalia letting out victorious peals of laughter until she noticed something change in the way Elba was holding her. It was almost as if Elba's arms, having been prepared to carry her, suddenly lost strength and now needed support. Dalia began pulling back, trying to look into Elba's face. Elba avoided it. "Elba," Dalia said, trying to disentangle herself, but Elba gripped her closer. It was about a minute before she loosened her grip. Dalia could hear her sniffing, feel something warm through her shirt.

"Elba," Dalia whispered slowly, "How about you?" She pulled her back and saw it written on Elba's face, which seemed all sunken in. The old Elba might've turned around so Dalia couldn't see. This Elba bit her lip and stared at the floor. "Fuck it," she said, sniffling, her fingers stabbing at the tears quickly. "I don't like school anyway."

"Elba," Dalia whispered softly, tears coming back to her.

Elba looked as if she had just lost fifty million dollars, her lower lip quivering. She covered her eyes with both hands and tried to make her face harden, taking a deep breath. "Nah," she said. "I gotta go."

"Elba, wait," Dalia said desperately. She reached out, but Elba spun away from her.

"I'll call you later," Elba said as she raced down the stairs, her sneakers thumping as if they belonged to a happy little kid on her way to play house.

Elba

Elba was lying in bed, not moving, hazy circles of sunlight
twirling designs on the far wall by the dresser. She closed her
eyes, then turned over, the bed still feeling warm. She didn't
get up. The baby was crying, tiny voice shrieking to her from
the living room. She tried to cover her ears with a pillow, but
nothing could blot out the commotion. The baby's screech was
a tiny air-raid siren wailing inside her skull, pulling, drawing
blood from her. She threw the pillow to the floor and stood up,
her black hair still springy and mussed from sleep. She didn't
bother to put on her slippers. The floor was so dirty she could
feel the sandy grit on her feet as she walked. She stopped by
the dresser, staring at herself in the mirror. She examined her
bare breasts, round and small and sullen, her fingers absently
playing with the nipples to make them erect. She wasn't
pleased with them. She had thought they would grow more
after she got pregnant, but nah, they shrunk back to their
original fucken size and now looked all small again. Budding
size. "I got virgin tits," she said aloud as the shrieking siren

intruded on her reflection, making her yell, "Dammit, I'm comin, I'm comin already!"

She moved away from the mirror, out of the small bedroom, pausing by the door to kill a huge roach that was scaling the wall. She tried hitting it with an empty paint can but missed. She jumped back and shrieked as the roach landed on the floor with a sick thump, its dizzying changes of direction making her panic. Elba dodged frantically as it raced past her. "Mothafucka!" she yelled. "Ya whole generation!"

She came over to the small blue crib standing in a pool of light by the old couch. She picked up the tiny bundle of baby nerves, her senses still pierced by the baby's cries; yet her irritation slowly faded, eddying waves of anger dissolving as she brought the baby up against her. Cradled in her arms, the baby relaxed, coiling tiny fat arms around her neck, stubby little fingers tangled in her hair. The baby was a part of her, and holding it soothed her, even though today she felt different. Her hands felt as if they would slip off her wrists. She didn't trust herself with the load, fearing it would slide through her grip and break like an egg on the floor.

"Why you such a problem, huh?" she asked in her best baby language. "You little sonofabitch, juss like ya father." Thinking of him suddenly made her nervous again. She checked the baby's diaper. "You got a little package f' mommy? No? Then be a good baby an stop cryin so much, ya gimme a headache." She put him back in the crib, tossing in a squeeze toy, her hand tapping a beat on the rim as she sang to him. He laughed, tiny eyes rolling, miniature hands grasping at her. She hated his eyes. She stared at them a bit and stopped singing.

"You look like ya fucken father, you know that? You came outta me, an you look more like him." She felt a sudden frustration come crashing down on her like a wave. The baby's face melted, becoming Danny's face. She had loved that face and had wanted to love that face forever. She had seen that face laugh and cry, but she had never seen it twisted with so much hatred and anger as it had been last night, when he stood by the front door with the police lock bar in his hand.

"Whachu think, huh? You think I don't work hard? All day long I'm workin, an you expeck me t' come home an stick aroun' like some fucken houseboy? Maybe you like this shit, but I don't." His face tensed with anger, eyes burning in a red liquid.

"Danny!" she had cried, eyes stinging. "Ya neva hea with me!" She had hated the way her voice sounded, all tinny and weak, as if she had been pleading.

Her words only made him angrier. He threw the police lock bar down with an ugly clatter and came toward her, eyes coated with something she couldn't see through.

"Yuh suppose t' be hea! Yuh the woman!" His voice rose. "You gotta stay home an bring up the baby! Thass it. You wanted marriage, you got it. Now I'm goin out!"

"For what? To drink more beer an smoke reefa? While I'm—"

"Damn you, yeah, yeah, yeah!" He towered over her, making her cringe inside as she stood against the tattered couch. "I got a right t' enjoy myself! I'm gonna drink beer an smoke, yeah! An if I want I'll come back an slap you aroun, too. You're my wife, dammit! You wanted t' be! Now yuh actin like you wanna start a revolution an shit! Don't get like that wit me, girl."

He came closer, grasped her by the arms, and pressed tightly as if he would squash her. She squirmed and began pleading because she couldn't recognize him. This was a complete stranger, a man who could murder her.

"Maybe you wanna be a mother," he sneered into her face, "but I don't wanna be no father. I din't wanna be. Yuh the one gotted pregnint. Yuh the one gotted us in this fucken mess. Dammit, lookit me when I talk!" He swung out at her, missed, pounding the couch with his rage. "You fucked up my life, you stupid bitch!"

"Oh, fuck you, fuck you, fuck you!" She pushed against him, squirming frantically until he released one of her arms. She hit out at him, smacking him on the chest. "I hope you die," she cried, "I hope you die!"

He struck her with his fist. She ducked too late and fell against the couch, where he cornered her and pounded her some more, until she lay motionless and staring.

"Don't ever tell me bout how I spend my money, don't fucken ever!" He ran from her, jumping over the couch, slamming the front door.

She stared down at the baby, who tugged on one of her fingers as if trying to pull it off. She felt at the bruise on her cheek with the other hand. The baby became a blur, her tears slapping against his bare tummy.

Six weeks of marriage. "Probation," he called it on one of those blurry red-framed nights when he stank of beer and she feared his alien eyes. Being together was now an assignment.

It hadn't been that way at first. They had dated like regular junior-high students, entranced by each other's bodies, jealous of them, eager to take possession. She was proud to have him, touched by those moments when he shyly became tender. He would clutch her on the street, pressing her eager curves against him, hands transfixed by the smoothness of her bare tummy and the softness of her waist as she pressed her ass against him.

"Whachu do if I love anotha girl?" he would ask playfully.

"I scratch ya eyes out, mothafucka," she'd say.

"You think I eva find a girl like you again?"

She'd give him a feline smile, pressing against his bulge.

"Why donchu tell me," she'd tease.

"I neva find anotha girl like you," he'd finally say, chewing on her neck, making her giggle and squirm with pleasure.

The Boy Without a Flag

She enjoyed two summers with him, grasping, holding, clutching as if she'd fall without him. There was nothing she wouldn't give him for his smile or wink or touch. They caressed each other in darkened movie theaters and deserted beaches.

"If only we had a car," Danny lamented as they sat on the stoop of her building on Tinton Avenue.

Two days after entering the eighth grade, after a few tokes on an old roach, Danny took her to the empty lot on Fox Street. Their sneakers struggled over jutting bricks and crackling wooden beams while a red sun splattered the sky and spilled through gaping windows.

"I picked a place out yesterday," he said like a newlywed. He lifted her up and carried her through dark hallways as he had seen men do in old movies on TV. He carried her down steps and over decaying planks of wood, nails sticking out of them like teeth.

He carried her over a cracked threshold. A lone candle stood in a rusted holder on the floor. Beside it was a mattress covered with a new flowery sheet. There was a pillow, too, and a box that softly whispered love songs, nothing but love songs. They toked on a joint and lay together, candle flame desperately dancing as breezes stroked it. The flame went out just as the sun set, and they lay locked tightly. They didn't notice the rotting wood smell at all.

They came to their little hideaway three or four times a week, loving furiously, until one strange morning when Elba felt sick. She threw up twice and felt dizzy. She began missing school, her body a stranger that throbbed and ached. Her mother seemed to know what was up.

"Did you eat something bad this week?" she asked in her sing-song Spanish.

"No."

"Maybe you drank something?"

"No, dammit, stop it with the third degree!"

Her anger and fear made her do weird shit, like slam doors and yell at her mother. She felt as if her body was no longer hers and someone else was taking it over from inside. She thought only of Danny, of his thick curly hair and that light beard that tickled her. She hid from the bad thoughts that tore at her until she missed her period. Then she went to Planned Parenthood. She saw a doctor who gave her a lecture about condoms. Then she had a test.

She couldn't bear to have Danny paw her. "What the fuck is wit'chu?" he asked, glaring at her as they sat on his two-dollar mattress. Her hands wrestled with each other in her lap. She turned her back to him. She felt ashamed. Guilty. "I went an got a tess," she said.

"A tess? Pregnint?" His voice scolded her. "How couldju let that happen?"

She began to cry. She wanted him to hold her, but he wasn't going to hold her. He paced up and down, yelling. She ran from him, fighting the tears as she stumbled through the lot.

"You sure it's me tha did it?" he yelled after her, making her feel cheap.

The doctor had talked about an abortion. She had raced out of the clinic.

"It's our baby," she said to Danny as he stood a step above her on the stoop of her building. "It's from us." She stretched out her well-tanned legs. He stared at them angrily, as if they had trapped him.

"Get a abortion."

"No," she replied firmly.

"Girl, abortion it!" He was losing patience. "I juss got in high school...I can't...juss get rid of it, man."

"It's from us. From me an you. I can't kill it." Her lower lip trembled. She turned from him so he wouldn't see her cry. "I thought you loved me," she whimpered.

He stared off into the street, at the streams of hydrant

water gurgling down the sewer. He suddenly walked away from her, jumping over the water, crossing the street without even looking back.

She didn't see him again for a year and five months. Her mother was sympathetic about it only because the same thing had pretty much happened to her. She tried spreading these sympathetic feelings to Elba's father with little success. He was upset, his large stoic face transformed into a seething red one. He no longer spoke, just shouted about the shame of what his family on the island thought of it all. Elba was out of school now and couldn't graduate with the rest of her class. In June, she was sitting by the window with her four-day-old son.

"What a beautiful baby," her mother would say, cradling it tenderly until Elba would take it from her.

It looks just like him, she'd think, her insides aching.

The baby was eight months old when he came back. He knocked on her door like a man who had returned to claim his fortune. Elba's mother was impressed by his business suit, talking to him in whispers in the kitchen while Elba sat in the living room. He stepped in almost fearfully.

"I wanna see my boy," he said, kneading his hands together. Elba stared at his shiny roach killers. She got up without looking at him and took him into her room, where the baby lay in a small crib. He looked at the baby and tried to wake it, then smiled at her. "I was wrong. I know that now. I wanna marry you an shit."

They got married.

Her mother was ecstatic, helping her pick out a pretty dress. The ceremony was quick and brief. There were no relatives. Rows of near-empty pews greeted them in the desolate Pentecostal church her mother attended. There was no honeymoon. Danny rented a two-room apartment in a private house on Kelly Street. He worked as a mechanic's assistant at Meineke on Bruckner Boulevard. Elba wasn't too impressed with any of it. The empty rooms depressed her.

Elba felt strange. She shared her body, felt his hands over her skin again, but there was a distance now. The sex was no longer carefree. There were arguments about the condoms. This forced her to do the pill ritual while he plunged into her. She resented having to be responsible. Sometimes she forgot about the pill. Sometimes his breath stank, his hands were too rough, his kisses brutal. He yelled at her to move, shake, yell, suck, bite, do this, do that, put on stockings, dammit. She felt trapped under him.

He hated the fact that she couldn't cook worth a fuck, but he resigned himself to it, making cracks as he dragged her down to the pizzeria, the baby content in his big-wheeled carriage. They'd make trips together to Longwood Avenue to hang out during those warm summer nights, but she knew that Danny longed to be out on the street without wife and carriage in tow. He began to stay out after work, not coming in until really late. She tried to live with it by going down herself, hanging out by the stoop with the baby and her pack of Marlboros. The carriage cut down her mobility. She couldn't run off and leave it parked by the curb like an idling Camaro, and while it was fine to sit and rap with friends on the stoop, by evening the friends would straggle off to the Bruckner Roller Disco, giving her the same line: "Too bad you can't come." They'd go; she'd be stranded, no choice but to wait for Danny, who sometimes came in so drunk that she'd settle for sleeping on the secondhand couch in the living room with the cushions that smelled like mothballs.

She'd stare out the window at the groups of kids hanging out, smoking and gyrating to music. They'd say, "Come on, *chica*, join us," but she'd shake her head sadly. Their laughter would drift up to her while she slept or washed dishes or changed little Danny's diapers. She felt old and lonely and abandoned, a lifer in a prison cell waiting for the chair.

The day she turned sixteen, Danny didn't even come home. He stumbled in at about six in the morning, outraged that she complained, storming off to work without so much as a kiss. The talk on the street was that he was spending his nights drinking at Los Chicos, staring at the flabby go-go girls. She complained. She was tired of getting fucked violently by him, so one night she screamed and pushed him off her. She told him she wasn't his fucking *puta* to just get fucked whenever he felt like it, that it was time he cut the shit and tried to grow up like she was trying to do, to accept his responsibilities and start spending more time with his wife and kid and less time at Los Chicos. It was a good speech, but she only got so far before he swung at her like a cornered animal, his blow throwing her off the bed.

The blow still stung, the sound of it reverberating in her head. She leaned on the crib and stared down at the baby without seeing him. She stormed away from the crib, pulse throbbing in her temples wildly, a terrible defiance taking hold of her. She peeled off her panties and turned on the shower, the room filling up with vaporous steam. The baby began to cry.

"Fuck you!" she screamed. "Fuck you! Getcha father to take care a you!"

She stepped into the dingy tub with the yellow stain by the drain and let the water beat on her, the slap of wetness drowning out the baby's cries. She scrubbed at her body as if erasing the memory of Danny's rough hands. When she shut off the water, she could hear the baby wailing loudly.

She scampered out of the tub, dripping water. She stared at the crib from the doorway, hands on her glossy wet hips. "Why doncha shut up?" she asked, but the baby wouldn't answer her so she went over to the stereo and turned it on full blast. Loud disco music drowned out the baby's cries, the throbbing rhythms making her writhe and spin. She swung her slim hips, bumping and grinding like a sex starlet turning men on in a nightclub, gyrating her girlish curves sensually to give those flabby *putonas* at the Los Chicos go-go a run for their money. A cool breeze made the curtains fly open, the frigid air striking her wetness like a startling caress. She dried herself off using a fresh towel from her drawer so she wouldn't end up using one he might've touched.

She began pulling clothes out of drawers, plunking them all over the bed as she swung her ass to the music. She debated whether she'd wear panties or not, decided against them, giggling and posing by the mirror. "Fuck it," she said, "juss fuck it."

She slipped on a pair of very dark panty hose and a pair of white short-shorts that she hadn't worn in ages. They were so tight they outlined her pussy, fabric creased in a triangle. Her ass cheeks showed provocatively, seeming to wink with every step. She put on a pair of high-heeled shoes that played up her long sexy legs. She hadn't worn them since junior high. Lastly, she added a bikini top that was too small, so she seemed to jiggle even though her tits weren't that big.

Commercials for mascara were blaring from the stereo. The baby was still screaming. She put down her lip gloss just to go over to the crib. She picked up the baby as if it were Danny. "You shut the fuck up!" she yelled. "I don't wanna hear you no more!" She dropped the baby into the crib. The fall seemed to stun him for a second, and he remained motionless and staring.

She walked away, back to the mirror as the baby began crying again. She added more makeup, the music animating her. She tied a red ribbon in her hair, swishing it around to see how it looked.

The baby was shrieking, its red face visible over the rim of the crib, creased like a battered peach. "If you shit yaself, tough!" she yelled. "Get ya father to take care a you!" The baby wailed louder, as if it understood. She locked the windows and left the stereo on. Opening the front door, she felt a refreshing coolness rush over her.

Two steps from the door she paused to listen, satisfied that she couldn't really hear the baby anymore as she made her way down the creaking stairs in her high heels.

Abraham Rodriguez, Jr., is a Puerto Rican-American who spends much of his time hanging out with kids in the same South Bronx neighborhood where he grew up. He brings his writing to them for critique, and their responses affirm that his stories are indeed mirror images of their own lives and the environment in which they live. "My writing has become more realistic and human through knowing these kids. Unfortunately, more involvement means more hurt. Some of my friends have been killed and it hurts me very much."

Rodriguez began writing when he was ten years old after his father, a poet, bought him his first typewriter. He dropped out of high school at sixteen because he was unchallenged and "tired of seeing the heroin addicts hanging out in the hallways." He continued writing and began writing songs and playing guitar. He earned his high school equivalency and attended City College of New York for four years, during which time he won First Prize in the Goodman Fund Short Story Awards two years in a row.

Rodriguez has become a more disciplined writer in the past few years and continues to write songs and play guitar in his punk rock band, Urgent Fury. However, in order to pay rent and eat, he takes odd jobs for two or three months, then lives off his savings for as long as possible. "I have stock jobbed, mail clerked, messengered, washed cleaned served delivered pressed stamped and baked. But, being broke is such an important part of being a writer."

Several of Rodriguez's stories have been published in magazines. *The Boy Without a Flag* is his first book.

The Boy Without a Flag was
designed and illustrated by R. W. Scholes,
typeset in Kabel and Walbaum
by Villager Graphics,
and printed by Thomson-Shore, Inc.

More Fiction from Milkweed Editions:

Agassiz: A Novel in Stories
by Sandra Birdsell

What We Save for Last: Stories
by Corinne Demas Bliss

Backbone: Short Stories
by Carol Bly

The Clay That Breathes: A Novella and Stories
by Catherine Browder

Street Games: A Neighborhood
stories by Rosellen Brown

Winter Roads, Summer Fields: Stories
by Marjorie Dorner

Blue Taxis: Stories about Africa
by Eileen Drew

Circe's Mountain: Stories
by Marie Luise Kaschnitz

Ganado Red: A Novella and Stories
by Susan Lowell

Tokens of Grace: A Novel in Stories
by Sheila O'Connor

Cracking India: A Novel
by Bapsi Sidhwa

The Crow Eaters: A Novel
by Bapsi Sidhwa

The Country I Come From: Stories
by Maura Stanton

Traveling Light: Monologues
by Jim Stowell

Aquaboogie: A Novel in Stories
by Susan Straight